AN AWFULLY LONELY PLACE

Linda Hudson Hoagland

DEDICATION

MICHAEL E. HUDSON

MATTHEW A. HUDSON

The loves of my life.

ACKNOWLEDGEMENTS

2002 - Novel – <u>An Awfully Lonely Place</u> (aka: <u>Deadly Secrets</u>) - Won Third Place in the Virginia Highlands Festival Creative Writing Contest

Publish America (America Star) of Baltimore for originally publishing this novel in 2008.

Victoria Fletcher, fellow author, for editing and formatting this book. She also developed the cover design for the book.

CHAPTER 1
MYSTERIOUSLY DISAPPEARED AND DIED

Secrets were a big part of my childhood as I was growing up. Now that I was an adult, the secrets were continuing to lurk around the edges of my life. I wanted to put an end to the secrets by discovering the truth.

I parked my car at the top of the hill overlooking my mother's dilapidated family home that was located in southwest Virginia amidst the green, lush, rolling hills of Richard County. I was afraid to drive over the road that went to the "Thompson Ruins" as I called the house and its surroundings, because of the deep ruts caused by a river of water draining down the hill every time it rained.

As I glanced up at the bright, cloudless, sunlit sky, I could see heat patterns rising from the ground traveling the rays to be lost in the overwhelming brightness.

I glanced to my right and saw what remained of the small farmhouse that had been built at the top of the hill long ago by a distant relative of mine for his new bride. The story goes that when the bride died at a young age, her husband abandoned the house. He couldn't bear to live in it without her.

On the left side from where I was standing stood the monolithic one room schoolhouse that my mother had once attended. It was in better shape, though that's not saying much, than the farmhouse because my uncle had been using it for storage.

Since I was a small child, I had wanted to know what he kept hidden in there. He never would let any of us- my parents, my brother, or me- go inside the place when we visited him.

As a little girl, I considered secrets fun, a game that adults played with kids to keep them interested in whatever they were doing at the time. When my Uncle Jim wouldn't let me discover the truth behind the secrets the old school house contained, my opinion of him changed. He became the mean uncle who didn't like me.

"It's too dangerous," he mumbled. "Junk piled all over the place. Could be rats and snakes in there."

"Why? It's just used for storage, right? There isn't any food in there, is there?" I asked when I had grown into a teenager.

"No, no. I don't want you in there," he replied in a forbidding, final tone.

My brother, who was not at all accustomed to the word 'no', tried a couple of times to break into the schoolhouse by picking the lock. He never could get the lock open and we never got inside to have a look see. He didn't want to break the lock because then Uncle Jim might suspect that he was the culprit.

When I climbed out of the car I left my car windows open to help circulate the heavy, oppressive heat and to keep the interior of the car at an almost tolerable level.

"Scram! Move it! Get out of here! Sca-a-a-at!" I shouted as I waved my arms at the cows headed in my direction to check out the bright, shiny vehicle. I had to chase them away or they would lick at the paint on the fenders, scratching the finish until a paint job would be needed.

The cows were in no hurry as they wandered towards the two lone trees that graced that portion of the hillside. They stopped under the trees, slapped their tails at the flies buzzing around their broad backsides, and stared at me with big, soft, brown eyes.

When I finished running around the car, looking like an idiot as I discouraged the cows, I was soaked with perspiration. I dreaded the walk down the hill to the old house where I would try to figure out why my Uncle Jim was dead.

I knew my ailing mother would have a million questions for me when I returned to Ohio. After all, it was my mother's baby brother that had been shot and killed.

My Uncle Jim definitely wasn't my favorite relative but I couldn't imagine anyone hating him enough to kill him.

"How could he live like this?" I asked myself every time I visited the old home place.

The roof of the L-shaped back porch was leaning precariously on each end towards the ground as only four of the six necessary poles supported it. The wood on the side of the house was grayed and full of decayed areas with some of it crumbling and falling to the ground. The chimney over the kitchen tilted to the side dangerously looking as if it would fall at any moment. The other chimney over the bedroom didn't look any better.

The new part of the structure was the kitchen that had a doorway to the back porch positioned in the longer part of the L and a doorway to the footpath that led to the outdoor bathroom facilities. That was a lonely, scary walk in the dead of night and an extremely cold walk in the snow covered winter. I didn't know what I might run into from foxes, to cows, to turkeys when I needed to follow the beaten path to the two-holer.

What was meant by "newer" was that it was an addition that was added a few years after the original house was built over one hundred years earlier. It was by no means new in that it was a cavernous room filled with a gigantic, wood-burning cook stove; a large, round, wooden table that tilted to one side following the slope of the floor; several mismatched wooden, ladder-backed, cane bottom chairs; a table that was built around the hand-powered water pump (that was a new addition since my last visit); a slate-topped table on which the tubs for washing hands and dishes were setting; and two old kitchen cabinets that held all the mismatched dishes and boxed or canned food necessary to accommodate a confirmed bachelor's style of dining.

Uncle Jim used only two rooms: those being the kitchen and the bedroom. They were located on the ground floor at each end of the L. To get to his bedroom from the kitchen, he either had to go outside and enter the hall from the second door that opened onto the porch turning to the right after he passed the staircase that led upstairs or, he could pass through what once was the formal living room crossing the hallway into the bedroom. The safest way to get from one end of the house to the other was to travel the first route, outside along the porch. The formal living room was filled with boxes of junk and newspapers that Uncle Jim had scavenged and saved over the years for who knew what reason. He had no desire to clean it up and make the entire downstairs habitable.

My mother had offered to help him sort and throw out junk each time she visited, but it did no good.

"Just leave it be. It's my home. You don't live here," he growled.

"I couldn't live here in this mess," my mother replied.

I always thought those conversations were ironic because my mother was the world's worst housekeeper. If I hadn't taken over many of the cleaning and straightening responsibilities when I was barely old enough, my dad would have left the family years earlier. My mother had never worked a day in her life outside the home, but she didn't work much at home either.

I smiled when I thought about my mother's offer to help.

My mother made Messy Marvin look good.

The smile was something new and wonderful. For years, all I could do was resent the responsibility of keeping my father home. That resentment faded with the passing years and the death of my father whom I loved very much.

Time was no ally to my mother. I was forced to move my mother into my home away from her friends and her son who were in southern Ohio.

My mother didn't like leaving her home but she had to be cared for much more closely than my brother thought necessary. The only alternative I had was to uproot my mother and take her under my wing in northern Ohio where I was living.

I continued with my mental tour through the "ruins" by going upstairs which consisted of two large bedrooms and a hallway that was also big enough to serve as a bedroom. All of the upstairs rooms were crammed full of boxes and junk except for small areas in each of the two bedrooms where a bed was set up with sheets, pillows, and blankets in place just in case he had an overnight visitor.

At the end of the downstairs hallway was another door that led to the front porch and the wooden swing.

I remembered swinging on that wooden swing that was suspended from the ceiling by chains as my mother and her grandmother sat on straight back wooden chairs they carried to the porch from the kitchen. Mother and grandmother were breaking green beans and getting them ready to can.

That was the day Lee and the ram had a confrontation.

Lee had a terrible habit of aggravating animals until they got so mad at him that they attacked or at least tried to attack him.

That day he picked a sheep to aggravate. He didn't know he had picked a male sheep that didn't like strangers in the least, especially little strangers. Lee was only about ten at the time and I was seven.

Anyway, while my mother and grandma were busy talking and breaking beans, the sounds of distant cries for help came filtering through their words.

"Do you hear something?" asked grandma as she stopped her work to listen.

"No…. yeah, I do. It sounds like Lee," said my mom as she sprang from the chair causing it to fall back against the side of the house.

Before my mom could run across the front porch, my grandma had jumped the steps and taken off in the direction of the sounds. She must have already figured out what was happening because she grabbed a piece of chopped wood with a big old nail sticking out of it when she ran past the woodpile.

"Help me, mommy, help me," cried Lee as the big ram kept butting him down each time he tried to scramble to his feet.

I was scared but I thought it was funny, too. Each time Lee would try to get up, the ram would bang against Lee's belly or back and knock him back down to the ground.

When grandma got close enough to the scene, she started swinging away at the ram with the wood and the nail.

Before long the ram ran off leaving grandma and mom to help Lee back to the house where they inspected his body for damage. He ended up with a couple of bruises but that was all.

I had to fight the need to laugh at him every time I saw him because I knew he would let me have it with his fist if he caught me laughing.

The next day I was bored and swinging on the wooden swing to keep myself occupied and out of trouble.

Lee must have slipped up behind me because I didn't see him. He threw something at the big old turkey gobbler and it ruffled it feathers up full array. That bird was enormous even when its feathers weren't ruffled.

I could tell it was mad, really mad. The beady black eye was staring at me from the side of its red skinned head. It looked like it was getting ready to fly across the wire fence and flog me.

That turkey was not only older than I was, it was a whole lot bigger than I was. I didn't want to get up close and personal with it by any means.

I stopped the movement of the swing and the big black gobbler spread its wings preparing itself for take off.

I jumped down from the swing and ran to the door yelling for my mom to help me.

When I was safely behind the screen door, I looked out again and saw Lee hiding in the bushes laughing.

I was mad at him, but I knew it wouldn't do any good to tell my mom and dad. They wouldn't do anything except to tell him not to tease the farm critters.

A few years later, I learned never to even think about sitting on the swing that still hung there because the floorboards under the swing had deteriorated to such a point that they would not support the slightest amount of weight or pressure.

"Uncle Jim, what happened here?" I asked aloud as I slowly walked from room to room to see if I could spot something out of the ordinary.

"Ellen…Ellen…are you here?" shouted a voice from the back porch.

"Yes sir, I'll be there in a minute," I answered as I hurriedly walked from the bedroom to the hall where I opened the door and let him enter.

"I'm really sorry about your uncle's death, Ellen," he said as he crossed the threshold.

"Thank you, sir," I answered not wanting to address him as 'preacher'. It didn't sound right rolling off my tongue, but that was what he was and how he was addressed. He was the preacher at the community church down the road a piece from my uncle's place.

We both stared at each other for a moment before I continued.

"The sheriff said that you were the one that found him."

"Yes, in the barn," he said as he cast his eyes away from me to the floor.

"What made you look there?" I probed as I tried to fit the pieces together.

"It's a long story," he said quietly not taking offense at the questions.

"Let's go sit in the kitchen while you tell it to me. It will be a lot more comfortable, I think," I said as I glanced around at the mess with which my uncle had lived.

"Well, Ellen, it started with his car. I found it in the church lot abandoned. At first, I didn't pay any attention to the fact that it was there. I thought maybe he had left it there because of car trouble; but after the second day and it still had not been moved, that's when I decided to do some snooping.

"It wasn't locked so I looked inside to see if I could find something that would let me know why it was still parked in the lot."

"Would you like something to drink?" I interrupted.

"A glass of cold water would be just fine," he said as he moved his hands across the table in front of him as if he were clearing away the dust and food crumbs.

It was a nervous gesture perhaps.

As I looked for a couple of glasses and worked the hand pump to force the water into one of the glasses, I studied the preacher.

He appeared to be in his late forties, which meant that his children were probably out of his home with families of their own. His wife was known to be the neighborhood gossip so it was likely that he would have heard all the rumors, if there were any, from her. The fact that I lived several hundred miles away from my uncle's place, in another state, provided me with a distinct disadvantage. I had no way of knowing the real truth so I was stuck with conjecture.

"Hello? Is anybody here?" shouted another voice as he made it known that he was present.

I peered out the kitchen door and shouted, "In the kitchen, Sheriff. Come on in."

The preacher stood up stretching his long, lanky body to its full height and searched my face for an explanation when the sheriff entered the room. Both men looked to be around the same age so I thought they might have a lot in common, might even be friends; but it didn't appear that way as I watched them greet each other.

"Preacher Johnson, I'm sorry I didn't tell you that the sheriff would be here, the same goes for you, Sheriff," I said hurriedly as I tried to relieve the tension that was filling the room.

I located another glass, filled it with cold water, and placed it in front of the sweating, overweight Sheriff Dunsmore because he looked as if he needed it; then, I told both men to sit and get comfortable.

"Preacher Johnson, would you start again? You left off at finding Uncle Jim's car," I said as I struggled to jump-start the conversation.

The preacher looked at me, then at the sheriff, and said, "Have you got anyone else coming?"

"No, no one," I answered. "It seemed to me that only the two of you, if you don't count the killer, can furnish answers to my questions. I'm sorry you're uncomfortable with the sheriff's presence."

"It's not that; I don't care if the sheriff is here. It's just that part of what I'm going to tell you may or may not be true and I don't want to get anyone into trouble unnecessarily."

"I understand, Preacher. I don't plan to run out and arrest everyone you mention," Sheriff Dunsmore said as sincerely as he could, looking as though he really wanted to hear what the preacher had to say.

"As I was telling Ellen, after the second day of seeing the abandoned car parked in the church lot, I decided to do some checking.

"It was unlocked so I opened the driver's side door and was hit in the face with a horrible odor. It wasn't just the smell of heat and normal odors from a closed car. Whatever it was smelled spoiled, like spoiled meat. I started to get into the driver's seat so I could reach over and open the glove compartment but the cover that was thrown over the seat slid against the plastic bag that was under it. When I picked up the cover and the plastic bag, I found the source of the horrible smell. It appeared to be blood that had spoiled from the heat. Because the plastic bag had been against the big wet spot, it prevented the air from drying the pool of blood absorbed into the cloth-covered seat. The blood was rancid and the smell was terrible. I held my breath, breathing only through my mouth and I continued to search.

"I still wanted to see who the car belonged to so I closed the door on that side and walked around to the passenger side.

"I looked in the glove compartment and found the vehicle registration which had your uncle's name on it.

Then I called the sheriff," he said as he glared at Sheriff Dunsmore.

I looked at the sheriff, which prompted him to begin his recitation.

"After the preacher got finished with his snooping in the car, any evidence we might have had with regard to fingerprints was obliterated," said the sheriff directing his antagonistic remarks toward Preacher Johnson.

"The registration was really the only useful thing discovered except that a ladies' watch was found lying on the floor in the back. Did your uncle have a lady friend?" questioned the sheriff as he looked at me.

"I don't know. He never mentioned one when mom and I visited him last spring or in the letters my mother received from him periodically. I've often wondered about him. Why he was such a loner? He didn't seem to trust anybody – not even family."

"Well," the sheriff continued, "the car hadn't been reported stolen, but there was plenty of reason to have the car towed to run some tests especially after we found the blood."

"What happened next?" I asked the sheriff.

"I guess you need to let me continue," said the preacher in a barely audible tone.

"Ellen, I knew your uncle in passing. He rarely came to church and he didn't participate in any of the social gatherings. He was a loner, a real hermit. He lived such an isolated, reclusive existence of his own making. He discouraged visitors with his rudeness and his shotgun.

"Nevertheless, I decided to drive here and see if he was all right. I was really worried about him.

"I knocked and knocked on the door. There was no answer and all the doors were locked. Your uncle never used to lock his doors so I've been told. I peeked in all the windows, but I saw nothing unusual inside.

One beautiful, summer weekend I decided to load up my suitcase and drive to southern Ohio to visit my mother and father. It would give me a break from the daily routine and a much-needed change of scenery.

When I arrived back home, I was shocked to find my front door standing open. I went inside and discovered most of my belongings were gone.

I went to the front door and looked toward my neighbor's home. Their house was completely empty.

It looked as though when they loaded their household items onto a truck, they also loaded mine onto the same truck.

I called the police and told them what I thought had happened.

After the police arrived at my house, I was told they would file a report but not to expect anything to come of it.

I checked with other neighbors and a man was seen in the area that day that didn't belong there. When he was described to me, I recognized him as my neighbor's cousin.

The first opportunity I had to glance at the newspaper was the following day after I had gone to work. I discovered that the same cousin of my neighbor had been arrested in one of the suburbs and was being held in jail for unpaid traffic violations.

I called the police department and told the officers, who were supposedly investigating the theft, where they could find the man who helped load the truck.

All they did was take the information. Nothing further was ever done. My file was one of many that weren't worth the effort.

****

I hoped Uncle Jim's death wouldn't be treated the same way.

"We found a red dress that definitely wasn't hers, meaning his mother's. We found a few fingerprints that we weren't able to match."

"Preacher, do you have any ideas?" I questioned.

"No, none, except my wife believes it was done by a woman who wanted his money," he answered meekly.

"What money?" I demanded.

"Everyone around here thought he had money because of the way he lived. They thought he was hoarding it and hiding it in this house somewhere."

"You've got to be kidding?" I shouted as I laughed uncontrollably.

"That's the rumor, Ellen. You know how people are when someone's a little different," added the embarrassed preacher.

"A little different? Uncle Jim was much more than a little different," I added.

I turned toward the sheriff and asked, "Did anyone ever see the woman?"

"No one that we questioned."

"Could the items, the dress and the watch, have been planted to divert suspicion?" I questioned.

"Yes, of course. It could have happened like that but we're going on the assumption that there was a woman who had heard the rumors; and, who for some unknown reason, stayed with your uncle a few nights. Perhaps she gave him a sob story about being hungry and not having any place to live. He probably would have taken in a good-looking woman. This is an awfully lonely place," answered the sheriff.

"Why did she kill him?"

"Maybe he caught on to what she was going. Maybe he caught her searching the place," added the preacher.

"All she had to do was leave," I stated.

"Was your uncle violent?" asked the preacher.

"Not that I know of. He was just unfriendly."

"Maybe he just lost it when he discovered what she was doing. He went after her and she had to fight back," put in the preacher.

"Maybe," I said doubtfully. "Didn't anyone hear a gunshot?" I asked as I groped for answers.

"No, Ellen. The nearest neighbor is up on top of the hill behind this house," answered the sheriff.

"Yeah, she's a distant cousin of mine, I think," I said as I listened intently to his explanation.

"Well, she works in the daytime. According to the county medical examiner, the shot was fired at around two in the afternoon. She wasn't home. Even if she had been home, she probably wouldn't have paid it any mind because your uncle liked to take pot shots at ground hogs and the like."

I got up from the table and refilled the water glasses.

"About the body, why was it in the barn?"

"I believe the strange woman killed him as he was sitting in the car," answered the sheriff. "He was shot in the neck in an upward angle with his own gun. He fell across the driver's seat, which is the reason for the blood in the car. She had to shove his body into the car but out of her way so she could drive. She then opened the barn door and drove the car into the barn where she pushed him out of the car onto the straw. There were signs that a vehicle had been there."

"Doesn't that angle indicate suicide?" I asked.

"Let me finish this and I'll go back to that question," continued the sheriff.

"Sure, okay," I answered as if I were being reprimanded.

"She went back to the house, gathered her belongings and what, if anything, of value she could find. Then left."

"She left without a trace? Why don't you think it was suicide?" I asked using an unbelieving tone.

"The way I see it," said Sheriff Dunsmore; "the body was moved too many times. There had to be a reason. The killer was looking for something, maybe the money. It looks to me like a murder and that's the way it will stay."

"The body didn't have to be moved by the killer. Someone could have found him slumped over in his car, pushed him out of the way, and driven his car to Uncle Jim's house where they threw him out into the barn so that same person could use the car to drive back to the church parking lot after the search for money was finished. Doesn't that sound like it could have happened?" I asked.

When neither man answered, I continued.

"That woman sure had to be strong to be pushing, pulling, and moving Uncle Jim's body around so much. He was over six feet tall and medium built. It had to be a real job for a woman," I said as I mulled over the sheriff's explanation. "Another question I have is how could you tell anybody was looking for anything? There is such a mess in this house at all times. How do you know anyone searched it?"

"You've got a point, Ellen. It looked a little more messed up than usual, if you know what I mean," added the sheriff.

"Preacher Johnson, what do you think?" I asked as I zeroed in on him with my eyes.

"I'd have to agree with the sheriff. There's no other logical explanation," he said as he looked directly into my eyes.

"Thank you, both of you, for coming here. My uncle was strange and it might have happened that way. Who knows? I'll have to accept what you're telling me and just go on. Maybe someday the answer will be here for everyone to see."

"Are you leaving for home soon?" asked the sheriff.

"Yes, this afternoon. Now that I have an explanation, I don't intend to stay in this house any longer than necessary."

"What are you going to do with your uncle's things?" asked the preacher.

"I don't know…maybe I'll let them stay here and mysteriously disappear and die, just like the killer and my uncle did."

A few days later after I had driven back to Cleveland and explained the findings to my mother, I received a telephone call from the sheriff telling me that the old Thompson home place had burned to the ground along with the old school house at the top of the hill. I had planned to go back to Virginia in the fall of the year to gather some of Uncle Jim's personal items that my mother had specifically requested, but now that was unnecessary.

"What caused the fire?" I asked skeptically.

"It was electrical. It started in the kitchen," sputtered the sheriff in his sorry explanation.

"What exactly was it? Do you know?"

"Must have been some kind of electrical appliance. You know the wiring was old, really old."

"What about the old school house? Why did it burn?"

"Vandalism, a bunch of teenagers running around loose around here. Parents don't keep track of them, you know."

"Thanks, sheriff, for calling me. I guess you haven't found the killer yet?"

"No, Ellen. I don't think there's much hope. I've got to go. This is long distance," he mumbled into the telephone.

"Bye," was all I got out before I heard the click of his hanging up.

Appliance? There were no outlets for appliances. The only electricity in the kitchen was for the overhead light fixture. The refrigerator was kept in another room because of the lack of outlets in the kitchen.

I figured that the fire had been set in both places so all traces of my Uncle Jim's past indiscretions would be removed. The house and its contents mysteriously disappeared and died just like Uncle Jim did.

The local authorities in Virginia were ignoring Uncle Jim's death because it was a boil they didn't want to lance. By burning the place down, they cleansed the land and the county of the problem. By not allowing the home place to be seen anymore, they removed its tie to Uncle Jim. Killing Uncle Jim eliminated this problem permanently.

The death of my uncle remained unsolved in Richard County.

I didn't believe a woman could have killed him because of all the moving of the body that was required.

I didn't believe a woman could get close enough to my Uncle Jim since his mother died, my grandmother, to have any type of intimate relationship because my Uncle Jim chose to share himself with teenage boys. I had never seen him in the company of a woman at any time that wasn't related to him by blood.

As far as the watch and red dress were concerned, Uncle Jim was a scavenger. He probably found those discarded items and took them to his car or his house. Once a junk collector always a junk collector. That's how he chose to live.

Perhaps my Uncle Jim finally had had enough of his strange, lonely life and decided to end it.

Perhaps someone had discovered his special liking for boys and was planning to expose him. Maybe a family member of one of the boys took exception to what was going on and decided to kill my Uncle Jim and permanently eliminate the problem.

My beliefs were leaning toward the fact that those holding enough power to sweep his death under the rug eliminated Uncle Jim.

No one who was local wanted to dig into the dirt to find the answers. No outsider like me would be welcomed to any answers to questions I might want to ask.

Just as it was when my furniture and clothing were stolen, the same would follow suit for my Uncle Jim's death.

All would remain silent forever, or so they thought.

CHAPTER 2
THE SEED IS PLANTED

"Mom, who do you think might have killed Uncle Jim?"

"I don't know, Ellen. It's been a long time since I lived with Jim in that house. I was so much older than he was. I left home and got married long before he grew up. I don't know who his friends were. How would I know the identity of his enemies?"

"What kind of a person was he when he was young?"

"What do you mean?"

"Did he ever have any girlfriends?"

"No, none that I noticed."

"Don't you think that's strange, Mom?"

"No, not particularly. He was barely in his teens when I left. We were poor, Ellen. We came from the wrong side of the tracks, you might say. Many people didn't associate with us for that reason."

"Is that the only reason?"

"Yes, of course," sputtered my mother angrily.

"Was grandma ever married?"

My mom hung her head. She didn't look at me and she didn't answer my question.

My grandmother, Molly was her first name, bore three children and none of them resembled each other in the least.

My mother, Winnie, was five feet four in height and almost the same measurements around. She had dark brown hair, in her youth, and bright blue eyes. She was

24

good looking despite her size, especially in her early twenties.

My Aunt Patti was five feet three with a slender build. She had curly to frizzy light red hair and she had a fiery temper that matched that red hair perfectly.

Uncle Jim was over six feet tall with brown hair and a large beak-shaped nose that really didn't detract from his appearance. He was country boy handsome.

From looking at the three siblings when they were in the same room, you would not be able to determine their relationship unless you already knew it.

I had never heard my mother talk about her father, my grandfather. Nor had I ever seen any evidence of a man who had lived in my grandmother's house other than my uncle.

As a child, I knew grandmothers usually came along with grandfathers but I didn't know enough to ask why I didn't have a grandfather on my mother's side of the family.

As I grew older and if I had any questions about my absent grandfather, I learned not to ask them. Everybody, including my mother, acted as if I had said something terrible and I was banished from the room the grown-ups were occupying until suppertime.

It was a secret that they weren't going to share with me, not ever.

I was an adult before my mother ever told me that she was born out of wedlock, as were Patti and Jim.

"Did you know who your father was?"

"Yes, he's a businessman and politician in Richard County. He is married and has several children."

"Did you ever meet him?"

"No."

"Did you ever want to?"

"Not really?"

"Why not?"

"If I wasn't good enough for him to see and claim as his then he wasn't good enough for me to meet and claim as my father."

Tears were forming in my mother's eyes and I knew it was time to stop talking about the past. That was about all of the discussion I ever got out of my mother concerning my absent grandfather.

The secret remained hidden.

I resented not knowing who my grandfather was. I resented my grandmother for putting my mother in the position she faced all through her childhood.

My mother was born in 1922 in a day and time when it was not good or understandable to have a child out of wedlock.

My grandmother had to be shamed by her neighbors and family for her indiscretion. That was bad enough for my grandmother, but when my mother became school age, she was teased unmercifully about being a bastard child.

It appeared that my grandmother really didn't give a damn about what her family and neighbors thought about her sleeping with a married man without the safety net of marriage because she became pregnant with my Aunt Patti and a third time with my Uncle Jim.

Maybe I should be looking at the sordid little tale from a different perspective, perhaps that of a woman who was so madly in love with a married man that she would do whatever it took to sustain his affection for her.

Then again, maybe my grandmother made her living by entertaining men. Maybe the entertaining of different men would explain why the brother and sisters did not resemble one another.

No one was going to tell me so I just had to invent a past for my grandmother. I would prefer to think that my grandmother loved the man who would be my grandfather so much that Molly would live with waiting for him to find time for her. When those small snatches of time occurred,

Molly would lie down for him without any regard to what the consequences might be.

I never liked my grandmother very much and I always believed the feeling was mutual.

My grandma was a tall, solidly built, stocky woman with the index finger on her left hand missing.

"What happened to grandma's finger?'

"She cut it off with an axe accidentally when she was chopping wood."

My father didn't care too much for my grandma either. You could tell that by the way he acted when he took the family to visit her. He was obligated to visit every other year for Winnie's sake.

On the off year, the family would go visit my dad's mother and father in West Virginia.

"How come grandma doesn't like me?"

"She likes you."

"If she likes me, how come when I'm around her she only talks about Sandy and Suzy?"

"She sees them much more often than she gets to see you. She knows them a lot better than she knows you. That's all."

I didn't accept the explanation as a child and I never accepted it as an adult.

That was all water under the bridge. My grandma was dead and Uncle Jim was dead. My grandma died of natural causes and Uncle Jim was shot by a person or persons unknown for a reason or reasons unknown.

"Mom, do you want to move to Virginia? Back to your land?"

"Why?"

"I was thinking about going back there and claiming the land that will be mine someday."

"Why would you want to do that?"

"You said my great-grandmother left the property Uncle Jim was living on to her grandchildren. When she did that in her Last Will and Testament, she passed over grandma who was your mother and the property then descended directly to you, Aunt Patti, and Uncle Jim."

"Yes, that's right."

"Then you have a one third interest in that land and now that Uncle Jim is dead and left no heirs, you own half of the land with your sister, Patti."

"I think I own all of the land."

"Why?"

"Before Jim died, he told me Patti signed her share over to him."

"So if something happens to you, that land comes to me. Right?"

"Yes, I think so."

"Let's move there, Mom. We can sell this house and buy a mobile home. We can set the mobile home up on the property and I'll get a job in one of the offices in town. What do you think?"

"I don't know, Ellen. I really don't want to go back there."

"Why? You would be closer to family and old friends. Wouldn't you like that?"

"I'll think about it."

"If we move to Virginia, maybe I can find out who killed Uncle Jim."

My mother glanced at me with a puzzled look on her face.

"You didn't like Jim."

"Yes, that's true but I think whoever killed him should have to pay. Don't you?"

I had nothing holding me in Ohio such as family and especially not work. I would give up the job I had in a second if I knew my mother would help me get through the rough spots.

After my dad died, my mother came to live with me. My mother couldn't drive and wasn't acquainted with a checkbook. My dad had always taken care of all expenses. Winnie was totally dependent on others.

I had always vowed that I would never be like my mother, being so dependent on my father for everything. My dad wasn't mean or stingy with my mom but Winnie couldn't do anything on her own without his input.

I had never married. I came close a couple of times, but plans were changed and the ceremony never happened.

In the back of my mind I always knew that my mother and I would grow old together. If that were the case and we were destined to grow old together, I wanted to do it somewhere else other than Ohio.

I was living in a city that was best for young adults who were affluent and willing to pay for everything the city had to offer.

I was getting older and no longer needed everything at my fingertips in a fast paced world.

I wanted life to slow down some so I could enjoy it. I wanted to savor the new experiences and the new relationships of my future.

I wanted to go back to the place that belonged to the white haired woman who always dressed in long black dresses and who was my great-grandmother.

Her name was Ella and she wore golden, round, wire-rimmed spectacles. She walked with a shuffle of her feet and she always had her hair pinned back in a bun at the nape of her neck. She seemed to have a strange smell floating around her that reminded me of hospitals and sick people.

She frightened me with her appearance. Her long black dresses seemed so out of place when I was a child.

My mom always told me never, never bother great-grandma. So, I didn't.

In my mind I was drawn to my home, my property. I wanted to go back and put the ghost of Uncle Jim to rest.

CHAPTER 3
CONVINCING MOM

Convincing my mother to go back to her roots was going to be harder than I had hoped.

For every reason I could think of for leaving Cleveland, my mother would come up with two reasons for staying put and living out the rest of her life away from bad memories and unkind people.

"What could they have done to you that was so bad?" I asked one day when I was overwhelmed with exasperation.

"The way they looked at me, the way they sniggered at me from behind hands held in front of their mouths, the way they ignored me like I wasn't there when something good was going to happen. Why should I want to see those ugly people who thought I was bad because my mother couldn't control her sex drive? Why should I relive that? You tell me, Ellen. Why should I want to even think about living through hell again?"

My mother burst into tears and I knew the subject was closed.

"Mom, I'm sorry. I just wanted to start over and live a better, more productive life. I wanted to live on the land that would be mine someday because I'm me, your daughter. I wanted to see the inheritance and make it better, but I won't go if you won't go. You know I can't leave you alone. I'll have to get my mind set on staying here for the rest of my days," I said as I tried to turn back on to my mother the guilt trip she had slathered onto me.

My mother didn't say a word. The guilt trip didn't work. She rose from her chair and walked slowly to her bedroom to read her romance novels and forget about the past and my desire to visit it.

My mother had high blood pressure that was controlled with medication. She appeared to be getting weaker and weaker with the passing of each day. On the whole, for a woman of seventy-five years, she was in surprisingly good health.

Four years earlier she had had several MIA's but had not been bothered with them since that time. My mother never believed she had suffered the mini-strokes because they were so short in duration.

I described to Winnie the contorted face, the slurred speech, the weak arm and claw like hand while the stroke was occurring. My mother totally denied doing anything like I described.

"I would have remembered that, Ellen. That couldn't have happened. You just made that up, didn't you?"

"No, I didn't. Why would I do that to you?"

"You want to get your hands on my money," my mother said as she stormed out of the room once again.

My mother didn't have much money, not even enough to bury her if she died the next day.

"Give it up, Ellen," I mumbled as I washed the dinner dishes. "She's not going to change her mind. The only way I would be able to go is over her dead body."

I forced my mind to dwell on another subject as I let the matter drop, at least for a few days.

I could always bring it up again when the dust settled.

I didn't get the chance to tackle the problem of trying to convince my mother to go back to her home place again.

When I walked into my mother's bedroom the next morning, she was lying across her bed at an awkward angle. I went to the side of her bed to wake her.

"Mom, wake up. You're about to fall off your bed," I said as I gently shook her.

My mother did not respond. She didn't wake up. She didn't move over on her bed. She did nothing but lie there. The only movements she made were the shallow intakes and expulsions of breath. I could barely see her chest rise with each intake of air.

"Mom, mom, wake up," I screamed as I reached for her telephone.

The telephone wasn't on her bedside table. I looked under the table and saw the instrument as it bleated its annoying tone for someone, anyone to pick it up and replace the receiver on its cradle.

I hung the receiver up onto the telephone base but left the telephone setting on the floor. I ran from my mother's bedroom to the kitchen where I called 9-1-1 for help.

"It's my mother. She's not moving. She's not waking up."

"Is she breathing?"

"Yes, just barely."

"What's the address, ma'am?"

I gave them the directions to my house and I paced the floor as I awaited the arrival of the ambulance.

After checking my mother's vital signs, the paramedics loaded her up immediately to be transported to the emergency room of the hospital about ten blocks from our house.

"What's wrong with her?" I asked the emergency room doctor when he finally made an appearance in the waiting room.

"Looks like a stroke. We will be running some more tests, but it doesn't look good. I'll tell you more later when I get some test results."

"Oh, God," I cried, "my arguing and badgering her about going back to Virginia did this to her."

"No, nothing you did or said to her caused this stroke. It was a long time in the making," explained the doctor. "I doubt you could have done anything to prevent it. Your mother was a ticking time bomb set to explode whenever her time expired."

I looked at the doctor and tried to smile. I wanted to believe what he said. I wanted to know that I hadn't caused my mother's stroke.

A couple of hours later, the doctor told me that my mother had had a massive stroke. He showed me the x-rays, pointing out the areas of destruction in her brain.

"You will probably want to consider signing the form requesting that we take no extraordinary measures to save your mother's life. When she wakes up, if she wakes up, she will most likely be a vegetable. She won't be able to function at any level on her own. She would have no quality of life. You wouldn't want that for her, would you?"

"No," I answered as I tried to hold back the tears.

A nurse brought me the form and I signed it, agonizing over its meaning, its finality.

After my mother was transferred to a room, I went home to shower and change clothes.

I hated the room my mother was in because it also represented the fact that there was no hope left. Each floor of the hospital had one of those rooms where there was an entranceway, a separate room, before you actually entered the room where the bed was located. The separate room served as a place for family members to wait for death. A place where they could cry and commiserate with each other over the fate of their loved one.

In my mother's case, I felt the room was a waste. I was the only family member who would be sitting and watching the machinery as it flashed my mother's vital signs constantly. I was the only member of my mother's family who would hold her hand and wait for the inevitable end to come.

The day after her stroke, I was talking to my mother and holding her hand.

"I love you, mom," I said as I squeezed her fingers gently.

When I started to place her hand on the bed, I felt my mother squeeze my fingers as if she were trying to comfort me.

Then nothing.

As each day passed, my mother slipped deeper and deeper into a coma until on the seventh day she was no more.

My mind stuck on the seven. It took seven days for God to complete the cycle of creating the heavens and the Earth, the universe, the world. It took seven days for my mother to die. How ironic that seemed to me.

I went about getting the necessary deeds done that would allow my mother to be buried next to my father in Alum Creek, West Virginia.

I was at the funeral home for the visitation in northern Ohio where my coworkers and friends paid their respects. The next day my mother's body was taken to West Virginia where my father's family paid their respects and my mother was lowered into the ground the following day.

I was stalwart and strong at each public appearance but I was a bundle of nerves and full of tears when I was alone.

I couldn't stay in that house without crying so I made up my mind to take the giant step on my own.

I was moving to Virginia to start over and to build a life for myself. While I was working at rebuilding and recycling my life, I would look into what ended Uncle Jim's life so abruptly.

CHAPTER 4
WHAT'S IN VIRGINIA?

I loved northern Ohio and I would truly miss it. It was rare for a non-native to develop such affection for the city. At least, it was among the people I knew and with whom I associated. That northern Ohio city was so fast-paced, exciting, and alive that it was like living in a whirling carousel whose speed was gradually building up to a faster and faster pace.

It was going to be difficult to take that first gigantic step down, away from the bright lights, the hypnotic musical tones, and the blurring beauty of the big city carousel.

I was getting older and needed to slow my pace through life. I wanted to enjoy my days without struggling to keep up. The forties weren't too old, but it was old enough for me to take stock of my life, especially after the death of my mother, and move ahead at a much more leisurely pace.

"Lee, can you help me move to Virginia?"

"Why do you want to do that?"

"I don't have anything holding me here. You have your own family and friends so you don't need me hanging around your neck like an albatross."

"What made you pick Virginia?"

"That's where we were born."

"Yeah, but we were small kids when we left Virginia. Where are you going in Virginia?"

"To Richard County, on the land we've inherited from mom."

"There's nothing there, is there? You told me the old house burned down. Where are you going to live?"

"I'll find a place to rent until I can get a mobile home set in place."

"You can afford that? Mom must have left you some money."

"No, no money. You know mom didn't have any money. I didn't have enough to bury her with. I'm going to be paying that bill for a long time to come. I could use a little help with it, you know."

"You know I don't have any money to pay on that. I'm barely paying my bills. If you're so broke, how are you going to do it?"

"Credit. I'll get me a job and use the land as collateral. I'll get it done somehow."

"Why?"

"Why what?"

"Why are you moving there? You'll be all alone in a new place. You won't know anybody."

"Yes, I will. I know the preacher and the sheriff."

"That's not what I mean."

"I know, but we didn't know anybody when we moved to northern Ohio."

"We were kids. We didn't have a choice. That was different."

"Not really. We survived as kids. I'm sure I can survive as an adult."

"What's the real reason?"

"I need a change, Lee. That's all."

"When are you wanting to move?"

"As soon as possible. Within the next couple of weeks, I hope."

"What's the hurry?"

"I'm going to Virginia, Lee. Why prolong the departure?"

"Okay. I'll see when I can get a couple of days off work. Are you going to rent a truck?"

"That's what I had in mind."

"Where are you going to store your stuff?"

"I thought the barn would be good. I'll buy a couple of padlocks. Nobody will even think there is anything in the barn because the house burned down. What do you think?"

"I guess it will be okay. Like I said, I'll see when I can get some time off work. Are you sure you want to do this?"

"Yes, Lee, I'm sure. Call me when you have the days, okay?"

"Sure. Bye, Ellen."

I finally said it out loud. I told my brother. The next step was to tell my boss. I hoped he would be happy for me but I had my doubts.

Mr. Hammond would not be as understanding as my brother would. He would probably take it as a personal insult that I was leaving him in the lurch without any reasonable, acceptable explanation as to why I would do such a crazy thing.

"Mr. Hammond, could I have a moment?" I asked as I walked into his office while gently tapping on his door with my hand.

He looked up from the letter he was reading and nodded.

I walked to the chair directly across from him and sat. I didn't want to stand over him as I told him I was going to leave. I wanted to be stationed at eye level so we, hopefully, would be on even footing.

"Mr. Hammond, I'm giving you my two weeks notice. I'm going to be moving to Virginia in the next couple of weeks so you will need to find a replacement for me."

By the time I had finished those few words, I was near tears.

"Moving to Virginia?" he asked in confusion.

"Yes."

"Why? What's in Virginia?"

"Family."

"Don't you have family here?"

"No one other than a brother."

"Have you got a job?"

"No, not yet."

"Have you got a place to live?"

"Well, not exactly. I'll be renting for a while."

"Two weeks? You're leaving in two weeks?"

"Yes, sir."

He looked down at the letter he had been reading and didn't say another word. I took it as a sign that I should leave.

He did take it as a personal affront because the next two weeks he avoided me like I was carrying the plague.

When I told him I was moving near family, I was glad he didn't pursue the matter further. Technically the only family I had in Richard County, Virginia, was my dead Uncle Jim. I would be moving closer to his grave was about all I could come up with as explanation for being closer to family.

Oh, I had distant cousins whom I didn't know and didn't particularly care to know in Richard County, but they were definitely not the reason I was moving to Virginia.

After I told Mr. Hammond of my departure plans, I knew I had to tell the man I had been dating for a couple of years.

I knew I wasn't going to get too much static from him because he was married. He would probably be relieved to see me go. He could then search for a new bed and younger thighs to crawl between.

The years had not been good for the relationship between Jack and me. The visits were fewer and further apart and the sex had definitely lost its luster.

Honestly, sex with Jack wasn't that good in the beginning. I was just so happy that he even considered sleeping with me; a chubby, short, dishwater blonde.

I would have done anything to maintain my relationship with Jack in the beginning. I was so in love with the thought of being in love.

I thought he was the answer to all of my problems in dealing with loneliness. It wasn't until I had committed my heart to the relationship with Jack that I discovered what loneliness truly was.

I went to the bar where I usually met Jack and waited for him to decide to show up, to decide that he had time to spend with me.

Monday night, I sat in the bar until nine o'clock. Then I went home thoroughly disgusted with him for not showing up and with myself for wasting my valuable time waiting for four hours in that bar.

I went to work the next morning and faced the world of avoidance from Mr. Hammond. He spoke to me only when necessary and then not always in a civil tone. It was going to be a long two weeks.

Tuesday evening at five o'clock I walked into the bar to hopefully tell Jack that I was leaving town, leaving the state, leaving the bed we shared for good.

Jack must have arrived at the bar long before five o'clock because by the time I arrived, he was loaded to the gills with beer, his favorite beverage.

When I entered the bar, he waved to me motioning for me to join him and his coworker cronies.

"What are you celebrating, Jack?" I asked as I laughed at his silly antics.

"It's Tuesday. We're celebrating Tuesday."

"Is that it?"

"Sure. We don't need a reason. We just like the beer," he said as he tried not to slur his words.

"Jack, I need to talk to you," I said in a whisper as I touched his arm to emphasize my urgency.

"Sure, what about?" he asked loudly.

"I'm not talking to everyone in this bar, Jack. I want to talk to you, alone. I need to tell you something, just you. It's important."

"You can say anything you want to say to me in front of my friends," he said with a flourish of his hand motioning to encompass all of the men surrounding him.

"Okay, Jack, if that's how you want it," I said with a sigh. "I'm leaving within the next couple of weeks. I will be moving to Virginia."

Jack blinked at me as he stood beside me. His head was turned towards me with his mouth open. He didn't say anything for a few moments as my words penetrated his beer-sotted brain.

I waited for him to speak.

"Virginia? What's in Virginia?"

"Not you."

"What do you mean? What are you trying to say?" he asked angrily. His fuse was short so I was almost glad we were having this conversation in a crowd.

"I'm moving to Virginia to get away from you and your lies. I want to start over with my life. I will use a nice clean slate on which to write the path to the rest of my life. I've spent too many years waiting for you to divorce your wife, as you told me you would do, and marry me."

"Ellen, you know…"

"Jack, I don't want to hear it anymore. My heart is tired of waiting to love and be loved. I've got to move on."

The people who were listening, Jack's cronies, were silent.

Jack was silent.

I was fighting the rising tide of tears I could feel filling my whole body and soul.

"Let's have a drink, Mike. Get us a round here," Jack shouted at the bartender. "Ellen, we'll talk about this later."

"No, we won't, Jack. We won't talk about this ever again."

I climbed down off the barstool and walked out the door.

I hoped it was over; no more Jack, no more tears, no more heartache.

That was not to be.

I cried as I tried to keep the car in the road driving home where I would cry some more.

"How could ending a bad-for-me relationship hurt so much?" I asked myself as I struggled to steer my car.

The house was so lonely and so disheveled because I had been packing and sealing boxes that I would store in the barn.

When I entered the house, I grabbed the television remote, a Coke, and a bag of potato chips. I was going to eat my chips and drink my Coke, which would serve as my supper. Then I could watch television until I got so sleepy that I had to go to bed. I wanted my mind to focus on the make-believe lives inside the television set.

My head was finally beginning to fall forward as my eyes closed momentarily.

"Got to go to bed," I whispered to no one. "Got to get some sleep for work tomorrow."

I walked to my bedroom and fell across my bed.

"Ellen, Ellen, open up!" came shouts from the direction of my front door.

"What?" I said as I tried to grab hold of wakefulness.

"Ellen, open your door!"

"What? Who?"

I ran to my front door where I saw Jack leaning against the door for support.

"Go away, Jack!" I whispered loudly.

"Open up, Ellen. I've got to talk to you."

He pounded again and again at my door. I knew he was going to wake up the neighborhood.

"Go away! I don't want to talk to you or to ever see you again?" I shouted back at him.

"Why? What happened? Did I do something wrong?" he continued to shout.

I jerked the door open to let him into the house. I was sure the neighbors would call the police if I didn't shut him up.

"Go sit down, Jack. You're too drunk to hold yourself up," I said with disgust.

"It never bothered you before, my drinking I mean," he slurred angrily.

"Yes it did. I just didn't tell you. I didn't want you to get mad at me."

"You didn't want me to get mad? Who are you kidding? You didn't want to lose a good thing – me. I'm your good thing."

"Not anymore, Jack. Go back to your wife. Show her what a good thing you are. I'm no longer interested."

Fury was evident in Jack's face. I was still standing so he forced himself up from the sofa so we would be standing toe to toe. He leaned back slightly and slapped me with all of the force he could muster.

I screamed and reached for the side of my face.

The scream must have brought Jack back to reality. He looked at me, turned on his heel, and walked out of the door.

The pain was raging and burning but it really didn't feel that bad. I could deal with it.

Jack was gone and out of my life forever.

I would really begin anew in Virginia. Nothing would draw me back to northern Ohio ever again. At least, Jack wouldn't be the reason if I ever decided to return.

CHAPTER 5
WATCHING OHIO SHRINK

The break from the world of city life was a long time coming and it would be permanent.

I was finally getting excited about my decision to change my life, to get a new life.

I had to wait three weeks before I could watch Ohio shrink to nothing in my rearview mirror. My brother wasn't able to schedule any days off until then.

We rented one of those big red and white trucks and loaded it to bursting at the seams. He drove the truck and towed his car for his return trip. I drove my car that was also packed to capacity and we traveled down the road on the eight-hour trip.

I was so glad I had a place to go. I had called the preacher and sheriff and asked them both to try and locate a place I could rent for a few months.

"Sheriff Dunsmore, this is Ellen Hutchins."

"Yes, Ellen. What can I do for you?"

"I'm planning to move to your area in a couple of weeks. I wanted to know if you know of any place that would be for rent."

"Moving here, Ellen?"

"Yes, sir. I'm looking for a place to live since the old home place burned to the ground. Do you know of any place?"

"No, no, not right off hand, but I'll keep an eye open and an ear to ground just in case I see or hear about anything. Where can I reach you?"

I gave him my home and work telephone numbers. Judging from his reaction over the telephone wires, I didn't expect him to return my call.

The next call I made was placed to Preacher Johnson.

"This is Ellen Hutchins."

"Yes, Ellen. How can I help you?"

"I'm moving to Richard County and I'm looking for a place to rent. Do you know of anything available?"

"Maybe, I think one of the people who attend my church might have a mobile home for rent. Is that okay?"

"If it's livable, it's okay. Have you seen the place?"

"Only from the outside. It's an old trailer, but the owners have taken care of it."

"Are you sure it's for rent?"

"No, I'm not sure, but I'll find out. Where can I reach you?"

I gave him both telephone numbers and felt certain that he would call me again.

A couple of long agonizing days passed before Preacher Johnson called me.

"Ellen, they haven't rented the trailer to anyone yet. I'll give you their telephone number and you can call them yourself."

"That's great, Preacher Johnson. Thanks for your help."

"That's okay. That's my job to help people, you know. Please call me Al or Allen. When are you moving here?"

"A couple of weeks. My brother is going to help me so he has to get some time off work. I have to finish up my two-week notice at work. You know, all that last minute stuff you have to do before you can load up and leave."

"It's a lot of work to move; especially when you're going out of state."

"Al, how's the family. I hope everyone is well."

"Fine, we're all just great. Well, I'd better go. See you soon, Ellen."

That was a nice friendly conversation, I thought, as I placed the receiver into its cradle. I wondered how long the friendliness would last after I got to Virginia.

I called the telephone number that Preacher Johnson, Al, had given me.

"Mr. Delbert Lawson?"

"Yes, you got him."

"I'm Ellen Hutchins. Preacher Johnson told you about me, I hope."

"Sure, he said you were interested in renting our trailer,errrr, mobile home."

"Yes sir, but I needed to know a few things first."

"Okay."

"How much is the rent?"

"Two hundred a month. It's a small trailer. We don't want to make a fortune on it. We just want to pay a couple of bills with the rent money."

"Is there anything wrong with it?"

"No, not really except that it's twenty years old. Everything still works though. There's heat, water, and electricity. You can install a phone and cable for the television after you move in if you want the place."

"Is there a security deposit?"

"No, just the first month's rent."

"What's your address so I can mail the two hundred dollars to you right away?"

"You don't want to see it?"

"I'd love to see it but I won't be there for a couple more weeks. I'll mail you the two hundred so you'll hold it for me and not let anyone else have it."

Mr. Lawson told me his address and said he would hold it for me for a week. If he hadn't received the check at the end of that week, he would try to rent it to someone else.

As soon as I hung up the telephone I wrote the check, addressed the envelope to which
I had affixed a stamp, and walked to the mailbox at the corner of my street.

Now, I had a place to go. I would store whatever I didn't need right away in the barn and I would move all the necessities into the mobile home.

I was getting excited about my new life.

"Lee, did you get a date yet?"

"Yeah, week after next. The boss wouldn't or couldn't schedule anything sooner."

"That's okay. Week after next is fine with me."

"Are you sure you want to do this?"

"Yes, I'm sure. I've already given my notice at work. I've rented a trailer in Virginia and I'm packing up. I couldn't be more sure about anything."

"Tell me again why you're moving there?"

"I need to start over and get away from this city. I love this city but I want to slow down a little."

"Are you running away from something?"

"No. Why would you say that?"

"This move; this decision is so sudden. Are you still seeing that guy, that Jack?'

"No, but he doesn't have anything to do with my moving to Virginia."

"When did you stop seeing him?"

"What does it matter?"

"I guess it doesn't matter. Week after next on the eighth, we'll get you moved then."

"That's great, Lee. Don't worry about me. I'll be okay. I really want to move and I'm not running away."

"Okay, Sis. See you."

I wished he would quit asking me about Jack and what my motives were for moving. I was ready to go, to start over, to build a new life.

The eighth arrived and I was packed and ready to go. Lee and I had loaded the truck the night before so there was nothing to stop me from leaving.

There were no friends throwing their bodies in the path the truck would follow. There was no Jack begging me to stay. Obviously, I was on my own to do whatever I wanted to do.

I ran to my car, jammed the key in the ignition, and took off like an excited teenager. I set my rearview mirror just right so I could see the city shrink in size and rapidly become a part of my past. It was a past I no longer needed and no longer wanted. I wanted to create a new past filled with new memories, good ones I hoped.

My mother's death gave me the freedom I needed to fill my life with new experiences, new places, new people, and hopefully lots and lots of new fun.

"Thanks, Mom. I love you and I always will," I said as I happily drove to my future.

CHAPTER 6
CONTRADICTIONS

There was no one to meet and greet us. Lee and I drove into town and followed the directions given to me over the telephone by Delbert Lawson that led us through the heart of town to the other end and into a rural area where neighbors were scattered and separated by sizeable distances.

We located the trailer I had rented by mail and found the key to the front door hidden under the wooden steps under a rock as Mr. Lawson had told me.

I knew the mobile home was old so I wasn't at all disappointed with its appearance. As a matter of fact, I was pleasantly surprised with the care that had been taken to maintain the outside appearance of the small trailer.

Inside the place smelled of cleaning fluids and polish. Everything shined and sparkled as bits of sunshine danced off the shining metal and glistening wood.

It was a wonderful, somewhat isolated, but a truly wonderful place to live.

Lee helped me unload my car and we carried in a few of the items from the truck. The trailer was furnished so most of my belongings were going to be stored in the barn. It was the very same barn where Uncle Jim's body had been found. That thought sent chills down my spine.

"What's wrong, Ellen" Lee asked when I shuddered trying to rid myself of the chill.

"I was just thinking about the barn. We're going to be storing all my stuff right where Uncle Jim's body was found. It gave me the chills thinking about it."

"You're not expecting any kind of trouble, are you?"

"No, what kind of trouble do you think there would be?"

"I don't know, maybe nothing. Who knows? They never found out who killed Uncle Jim, did they?"

"I don't think they looked very hard if you want to know the truth."

"Why do you think that?"

"It's just a feeling I have. You know Uncle Jim was not the friendliest person that ever lived. Besides that, I'm sure the Bible-belters around here probably condemned him because of his keeping company with teenage boys. If we think he was strange and we're his relatives, what do you think non-family members would believe?"

"You've got a point. Still, no matter what they thought, that shouldn't stop them from looking for his killer."

"You'd think so, wouldn't you?"

We walked through the house and I told Lee he could have the bed when the time arrived. I would sleep on the sofa.

"Let's go over to the property and check out the barn before it gets dark."

"That's a good idea. I want to make sure I can get the truck down the hill without any problem."

Even though we had driven several hours already, we jumped into my car to go exploring without any grumbling.

It was a long thirty-minute drive from where the trailer was located. We had to drive back into town and then through it retracing the route that led us to the trailer. When we got to the other side of town, we drove another couple of miles until we reached the old Elk Mountain School where we turned right. We traveled that road for a couple of miles and then turned again to the left onto a gravel road for another mile and a half. That gravel road took us to a second gravel road and a gate.

I was driving so Lee scrambled out of the car and opened the gate so I could drive through and wait for him to close the gate.

Uncle Jim had been leasing the land for grazing by the neighbor's cattle so all gates had to remain closed unless a cattle guard had been installed at the gate. Uncle Jim wouldn't have footed the bill for anything as extravagant as a cattle guard so opening and closing the gate was mandatory.

Lee jumped back into the car and I followed the tire-rutted road that wound around a small rise and crested another rise before dropping down into the valley where the old house had once stood. We passed the burned out remains of the old schoolhouse that stood atop the first rise.

My car was built low to the ground so I knew I could do some damage under the car if I wasn't careful.

I tried to steer my wheels with the right ones on the raised center mound and the left wheels on the outside lip of the worn grooves of cars and trucks from days long past.

The ride down the hill was difficult because I had to fight the steering wheel that seemed to have a mind if its own. It seemed to choose the ruts as the path of least resistance.

The car wobbled and shook and bobbed up and down occasionally scraping its bottom on the hard ground, but we finally made it down the hill close to where the house had burned to the ground.

We both climbed out of the car to look at the charred remains of the material representation of our ancestors.

The two chimneys, one from the kitchen and one from Uncle Jim's bedroom stood tall like blackened tombstones marking the grave.

Lee and I walked to the area that once led to the L-shaped back porch.

"This place was old, Ellen, and nothing but a tinder box. But look at how badly it burned. Even the porch roofs were burned to a crisp. The fire actually melted the tin roof. It had to really burn hot to leave everything in cinders.

"You think it might have had some help?'

"Looks like it to me but I'm no expert. I've only seen remains of houses that supposedly had been torched in northern Ohio."

"Why would you know the difference?"

"Curiosity. If I heard a rumor that the fire had been set, I would check it out. Morbid, isn't it?"

"Yeah, a little."

Lee grabbed a stick and started poking around in the ashes.

"Be careful, Lee," I whispered.

"Look, Ellen, the out building didn't burn,"

The outbuilding was up the hill to our left as we stood facing the porch.

"I wonder why they didn't burn it down."

"Probably nothing in it. Uncle Jim didn't keep it locked so I guess it was mostly empty. Want to take a look?"

"We'll do that tomorrow after we bring the truck here. Right now we've got to look at the barn before it gets too dark for us to drive out of here."

We climbed back into the car and turned down the wide path that was probably a wagon road from the past.

About half way down the slightly sloping path, I stopped the car directly in front of the barn. We scrambled out of the car and sneaked up to the barn looking as if we expected something to jump out and grab us.

We carefully stepped closer and closer to the barn. We hunkered down as if that were going to prevent us from being seen by an unknown trespasser waiting in the barn.

I realized how stupid we looked and how dumb we were acting; two grown, forty-something adults, acting like frightened children.

"It's just an empty barn, Lee. Why are we acting like this?"

"Because Uncle Jim's body was found here. It was, wasn't it?"

"That's what Preacher Johnson said. But that has long passed now. We shouldn't be scared of an empty barn."

"Right," said Lee skeptically.

We entered the barn after we convinced ourselves that we should straighten up our weak backbones and forge ahead.

We could see that many people had been inside searching. The straw had been raked and an area on the dirt floor looked as if it had been cordoned off to block the entrance to that particular area.

There was no blood, no trace of Uncle Jim's body, but I knew the cordoned area was where the body was found.

At that point in time, we weren't disturbing any evidence because the barn had been thoroughly searched by someone. I assumed the legal authorities had done their job adequately to the point of obtaining evidence located around dead Uncle Jim.

We walked around pushing against the walls, checking the doors, searching for weaknesses that would admit a thief. After all, I was planning to store the material aspects of my life in that barn. I wanted my things to be as safe as possible. I didn't want everything I owned to fall into the hands of a stranger.

"It's funny, isn't it, Lee?"

"What's funny?"

"That Uncle Jim would have a barn that was in one hundred percent better condition than his house and that's not saying much. The barn is old, but, at least, it's still standing."

"You sure you want to put your stuff in here?"

"I don't have a choice. My furniture isn't going to fit into a furnished mobile home."

"How are you going to keep on eye on it?"

"I'll just have to drive here every other day until I can get everything out of here."

"I hope you know what you're doing."

"So do I, brother dear, so do I."

The hasps on the door appeared sturdy and the walls were sufficiently solid, I hoped.

"We'd better get out of here before it gets dark."

"Okay, let's go. We'll bring the truck here and unload it tomorrow first thing in the morning."

We were both exhausted when we reached the trailer, I curled up on the sofa and told Lee to sleep in the bedroom.

The next morning at dawn I was trying to move around quietly so Lee could sleep a little longer. He had the long drive ahead of him back to Ohio after we unloaded the truck and dropped it off at the closest rental facility.

I was feeling all kinds of contradictions. I was happy about starting over but I was also scared of it.

"What if I've made a mistake? I've got to tough it out. I can't afford to do anything else," I told myself in my mind.

"What if I find out what really happened to Uncle Jim? Why won't the authorities do any more investigating? Who burned the place down? Why? What if I get into something I can't handle? What then? I don't know anybody around here well enough to ask for help. Am I getting into something too dangerous to mess with?"

My mind was swirling with questions.

"Ellen?" I looked up to see my brother walking into the living room.

"Yeah?"

"What time is it?"

"A little after seven."

"We need to get started so I can finish up with you and go on home."

"Okay. I'll grab my jeans and we can stop to get something to eat on the way to the barn."

I parked my car at the top of the hill and climbed into the truck with Lee for the ride down the hill to the barn. Even though the truck was enormous, it was easier to drive down the hill than my car would be because it stood higher off the ground. It didn't bottom out like my car did.

Lee and I hauled boxes and furniture into the barn for most of the morning. The locks were placed on the doors and we headed up the hill back to the trailer where I got my car and followed him to the drop off point for the truck.

Lee was finally in his car and ready to leave at one in the afternoon.

"Stop and walk around if you get tired," I shouted at him as he backed his car out of my driveway. "Thanks for your help. I couldn't have done it without you."

He waved and was on his way,

I waved back at him as I stood crying at the end of the driveway.

I didn't know when we would be able to visit each other again and that thought made me very sad.

CHAPTER 7
MY NEW LIFE

I started my new life by unpacking my clothes, changing the sheets on the bed, and generally straightening up what my brother and I had messed up.

I went to my car and started driving around looking for a grocery store. My cupboards were bare.

Things had changed so much from when I was a child visiting my grandmother. I remembered all of them: my brother, mom and dad, grandma, and Uncle Jim, loading up in our car to go shopping at the Piggly Wiggly. I always loved the name of that grocery store.

The Piggly Wiggly was no more; at least, not in the little town of Lebanon. I was so disappointed with the demise of the store.

Directly across from the empty hulk where Piggly Wiggly used to live was the A-Mart Food Store that soaked up all of Piggly Wiggly's customers. Sometimes progress can be a truly harsh reality.

I drove further down the road until I came to a sign that pointed into the direction of Food Lion. I was familiar with that grocery chain so that's where I wanted to shop.

There weren't very many people in the store doing their shopping. I guessed it was the wrong time of the day for many people in this small town to be out and about.

I did notice that I was being noticed. Every time I glanced up, I saw a store employee watching me. I felt like I was the only fish in the fish bowl with all eyes upon me watching my every move. I certainly hoped that they didn't think I was there to case the joint for a robbery. I figured it was only because I was a stranger in town.

I was the focal point of any and all discussions in the store. I was driving a car with Ohio plates that was noticed by a stock boy who had been gathering the grocery carts that were scattered throughout the parking lot.

My checks were Ohio checks so I knew better than to present one for payment of my groceries. I offered cash instead.

"You're new around here, aren't you?"

"In a way," I answered as I tried to avoid a long, nosey conversation.

"I know most everybody that comes in here. I've never seen you before," probed the young female cashier.

"That's possible," I said, "I never shopped in this store before today."

I reached for my change and out the door I walked pushing my grocery cart filled with bagged merchandise.

I wanted to meet people, but I wanted to be discreet. Becoming best friends with a grocery clerk in this small town was like advertising your life on one of those enormous road signs. I wasn't ready for that.

It was late Friday night and it looked as if the town had rolled up its sidewalks and taken them in for the night. Nobody was out except me, the new woman in town, who was taking my groceries to my new home to live my new life.

Saturday morning arrived and I had nothing to do. I needed a telephone and cable but I couldn't call the service providers until Monday morning. I could read which was what I did quite often but I was too restless for reading.

I opted to drive to the old home place and do some snooping. I wanted to check on my belongings, too, but my main objective was to snoop around and see if I could turn over some rocks.

I really wanted to know why Uncle Jim died such a violent death.

I wanted to know who could hate him so much.

I wanted to know why his killer hadn't been found.

I wanted to know why they weren't investigating anymore."

The day was beautiful. I was looking forward to being outside, strolling around my property, taking in the beauty of the area. It was really nice to think about it. It was my property.

"It's my land, my very own real estate," I said aloud as I drove my car.

I followed the same route that I had taken when my brother was with me. I didn't know of any alternate routes to be taken.

After leaving the car, opening the gate, entering the car again to drive through the gate area, then leaving the car to close the gate, I had no doubt that a cattle guard should be installed to eliminate that problem. If it were raining, a body could drown before the gate duties had ended. With cattle roaming freely on the property, I couldn't chance leaving the gate standing open. That was one problem that would be added to my loan request, I definitely needed a cattle guard.

Of course, I could make an entrance to the property from the lower end of the wagon path that went past the barn leading to the gravel road that continued a circuitous route around the property from the bottom of the hill. If I decided to use that ingress onto the property, a large drainage tile or a small bridge would be necessary to allow the creek to flow through the tile permitting vehicle access over the top or allowing access over the flowing creek by using a bridge.

I preferred to enter from the creek end of the property but it would really depend on how much the cost would be to make the property accessible versus how much

I would be allowed to borrow for land improvements from a bank.

After closing the gate, I drove up next to the ashes of the old school house.

I remembered the grayed, steepled building standing on the rise inside the gate as exhibiting the resemblance to a prim, proper, stand-up-straight, long-skirted school marm with her hair piled up on her head in a fashionable style of the time period.

The door to the old school house never exhibited the welcoming smile of a pleasurable entrance to the room inside. The windows were boarded up from the inside allowing no sparkle of happiness to be seen by passersby. It looked as if the stern school marm was unhappy without any charges to care for and teach.

I was going to miss the gray lady from the past.

I grabbed a stick and poked around in the charred wood and ashes to see if I could figure out what Uncle Jim had kept hidden from us in that old school house for those many years.

He was so good at keeping secrets. My whole family was good at keeping secrets.

The old school marm wasn't going to give away Uncle Jim's secrets. Only bits and pieces of metal, most of it melted and out of identifiable shape, could be found in the ashes. There was nothing there that would help me with why he was killed.

I left my car parked beside the remains of the schoolhouse and with stick in hand I proceeded to walk down the hill to the blackened earth that once was a house.

I knew the fire had been set that burned the house. No one was going to be able to convince me otherwise because I also knew there were no electrical appliances in the house that could take the blame.

Who and why? I couldn't imagine but I was going to poke and prod into everything and everyone related to Uncle Jim's life to find an answer.

The remains of the house gave me no new information so I dropped the stick I had been carrying and walked over to the outbuilding that had not burned.

I didn't expect to find anything in it. Like my brother said, Uncle Jim didn't keep it locked so nothing valuable was stored in there.

Entering the building after being in the bright sunlight caused sight problems. I couldn't see where I was going. I didn't want to walk further inside until my eyes adjusted to the darkness. I was afraid my foot would step on or brush against something that would send my imagination racing. I was also afraid that I might fall through the floor if it was weak. I could possibly break a leg or worse.

"Then what would I do? There was no one around to help me. No one would be able to hear me unless the wind was blowing just right and it might carry my plaintiff cries up the hill behind what used to be the home place to the cousin who lived at the top of the hill," I said softly as I tried to bolster my own courage.

Finally, my eyes were beginning to focus to the darkness. I warily took a step forward as I listened for the sounds of wood splitting.

No sounds, not even a creak came from where I had placed my foot.

I looked around and saw the leavings of mice, I hoped, rather than rats.

In the corner furthest from me I saw what looked to be a makeshift bed. Someone had been sleeping in this building.

"Who could that have been?" I wondered. "Will that someone come back to his bedding? He might be lurking around outside waiting for me to leave."

I looked around again. I needed something for protection in case he did come back to his bed. I angled my head so I could hear the slightest breath or snap of a twig.

"Did I hear something? Or was that my own active imagination?" I asked softly.

I reached for a piece of wood that was propped against the wall. The wood was graying and old. When I applied a little pressure to it, it snapped like a twig.

"Now what?" I said aloud as I looked again for some kind of defensive weapon.

Nothing, I couldn't find anything I could swing at or hit an attacker with so that I could run.

"I'd better get out of here," I said in a normal tone of voice.

Subconsciously I must have been trying to let the trespasser know that I was in the building and that he should disappear before I walked through the door.

I heard nothing; no running, no heavy breathing, no sounds of anyone leaving the area.

I stepped into the sunlight and was startled by its brilliance, but I wasn't going to allow that to impede my progress if I needed to run.

Nothing unusual was occurring around me. I heaved a big sigh and headed for the barn. I was humming as I walked. It was a quiet, pleasant hum. It was a ready-or-not-here-I-come hum. It was a warning of sorts, telling anyone hanging around that I was on my way.

CHAPTER 8
I HUMMED

I hummed all the way to the barn. I hummed even louder while I stood outside of the front doors to the barn as I searched for the keys that I had stuffed into my pockets that would unlock the padlocks.

I slowly inserted a key into the padlock, turning it to force the lock to snap open.

I removed the lock from the metal loop on which it hung. I held the lock in my hand as I pulled the barn door open so I could look inside.

"Everything looks fine," I said as I walked further into the barn.

There was no electricity in the barn so the corners remained in shadows as I looked around.

"Why didn't I bring a flashlight?"

I hadn't really expected the barn to be dark inside because the sun was shining so brightly outside. It hadn't occurred to me that the barn had been closed up tight with little, if any, light filtering through cracks around the doors and boarded windows.

I opened the barn doors wide to admit as much light as possible before I checked further into the barn.

My belongings had been placed directly in the middle of the large open area at the center of the barn. We did that to keep my things away from the wet of rain that might seep in around the ground floor near the walls.

I walked toward the pile of items and turned to my right so I could walk completely around and check everything.

As soon as I reached the backside of the boxes that were stacked higher than my head, I heard a noise.

"Is anyone there?" I whispered as I ducked down behind the boxes.

No answer.

I stealthily moved further around the boxes so I could try to peek towards the door. As I leaned forward, boxes started falling at me from behind.

"Hey, stop it!" I screamed as I tried to scramble out of the way of the falling boxes.

More boxes fell towards me. They felt like they were being thrown at me.

I didn't scream anymore. I was terrified but I didn't want to waste my breath screaming.

I raced to the open doors and ran out of the barn.

"Where can I go?"

I didn't think I could run fast enough to get far enough away from my attacker and get up the hill to my car.

I started running down the wagon road to the creek. There was a wooded area near the creek. I could hide there until I could figure out how to get back to my car.

I was running as fast as my chubby short legs could carry me. I could hear my attacker behind me pounding his feet against the ground as he ran after me.

There was a rise, a ground swell, to my right that led eventually to the mountain that towered over the valley where my property was located.

I knew that before I got to the creek I would have to climb a fence. I didn't think I had enough time to do that.

I turned my running body to the right and faced the struggle of running up hill. I was so winded that I couldn't breathe. I stopped as I clutched my sides with both hands. I turned around to see my attacker.

"Where are you?" I whispered as I struggled for air. "I want to see who you are. Where did you go?"

After I stopped talking to myself and my breathing had slowed a bit, I could hear him running.

I started running again up the rising hillside towards the cover of the wooded mountain.

I knew I couldn't go up on the mountain, not alone anyway. If I did, I would never get back down. My sense of direction didn't exist. I could be lost for days before finding my way back to my car. I wasn't lost yet, but it wasn't going to take much to get me confused.

I saw the dark uninviting beginnings of the forest. I plunged into the darkness and ducked down, turning around so I could see if I was still being chased.

I looked up and all I could see were the leaves and branches of overhanging trees. They served as a roof blotting out the sun.

I looked into the direction that I expected to see my attacker.

I saw no one.

I heard no footfalls or heavy breathing.

"Where did you go?"

I sat on the ground and leaned against a tree. I needed to rest. I needed to get clear in my mind what I had to do next.

"What do I do now? How am I going to get back to my car? How am I going to lock the barn? Why am I being chased? Have I happened upon a homeless person? If so, why is he staying here?" I questioned myself.

It was five in the afternoon. It wouldn't be fully dark for at least a couple more hours.

I decided to wait until dusk to make my way back down the hill into the valley where I would climb the fence and cross the creek to get to the gravel road. I would follow the road to the turn off that led to my parked car and get the hell out of there.

I would get help and come back another day to lock the barn. I would just have to take my chances with losing everything I owned.

I knew if my attacker had continued to follow me, he would have been able to find me easily. The tall grass and weeds I ran through folded over under my feet blazing a trail a child could follow. In a few hours that path would disappear because the grass that wasn't broken, only bent, would spring back into place obliterating the trail.

"Why had he stopped chasing me?" I whispered to the shadows.

I climbed a little further up the slope so I could sit and look down on the path below me. I sat there watching and wondering until it was seven o'clock and the sun had dipped down below the mountaintop. It wasn't completely dark yet, but it was dark enough to make it difficult to see for long distances.

When I reached the open areas, I hunkered down a bit hoping I wouldn't be seen at all because of the brush growing on the slopes.

I heard no one.

I saw no one.

When I reached the wagon path I stopped to listen and look.

"Where is he?" I asked loudly.

I heard nothing and saw no one so I decided to follow the wagon path close to the ground to get to my car. That would mean I would have to pass the barn, but it was the quickest way to get out of there.

The wind started blowing making noises that caused me to stop in my tracks.

"Was that the wind? Or, is he back?"

The noises were ahead of me and the gravel road was behind me. I turned toward the direction of the road and started running again.

When I got to the fence I climbed over it, slid down the creek bank, and scrambled up the other side to get to the gravel road.

It was dark but a little piece of a moon and sparkling stars provided enough light so I could follow the road to get to my car.

I never realized until then how isolated and lonely that area of Richard County was until I was walking though it in the dark of night.

I kept to the side of the road in case I heard the footfalls of my attacker coming up behind me.

I hadn't realized how long the road was that circled the hill, or perhaps I should describe it as ridge of hills, that surrounded that end of my property.

Maybe it wasn't as long as my scared mind made it out to be, but I wasn't going to quibble over how long, long was.

No cars passed at any time during the frightening walk. I had hoped a car would come by because I would have flagged it down and gotten a ride back to my car as well as having the company of another human being. I thought, in this instance, there would be safety in numbers.

When I reached the turn off that led to the gate, I heard someone walking.

I ran to the gate and opened it letting it swing wildly as it banged against the bank of hillside where the gate had been anchored. I ran to my car, pausing only to get my car keys from the pocket of my jeans. I was shaking so badly that I had trouble trying to get the key into the door lock.

"Oh, God, let me get out of here," I prayed as I finally forced the key into the lock.

I jumped into my car, started the engine, flicked on the lights, and roared out of there. I left the gate swinging

in the wind. I didn't care if every cow in Richard County
got out onto the road.

CHAPTER 9
THANKS FOR NOTHING

I was home in my rented trailer. I no longer had to run from an attacker. I no longer had to hide for fear of being chased, or worse, for fear of being killed.

"But why? Why is this happening to me? I haven't been in town long enough to question anyone about Uncle Jim. If this attack is related to his death, how did the attacker know about me? How did he discover who I am? What is he afraid that I am going to find out about all of this?" swirled the never ending questions through my mind.

Too many questions were swirling around in my head. None of this mess was making any sense to me.

I wanted to call the sheriff and let him in on what had been happening but I didn't have a telephone, not yet anyway.

I read for most of the morning on Sunday. With no television to watch and no telephone to use, reading was about the only form of entertainment left for me.

The restlessness was getting to me, big time.

I jumped into my car and drove to the sheriff's office to talk to whomever might be on duty. I wanted to see if someone would go with me to lock the barn door. I had been chased once, when I was alone. I wanted to find out if that would happen again if I had company with me in the form of a uniformed law officer.

"Is Sheriff Dunsmore around?"

"No, he won't be in until Monday. I'm Deputy Martin. Is there something I can do for you?"

"Well, I don't know. I really need some help with locking a barn door."

"Help with what?" asked the youthful male as he smiled at me in a condescending fashion.

"It's long story, but what I need is for someone to go with me or to meet me at my property on Dry Branch to accompany me to the barn so I can lock it."

"Why do you need an officer with you?"

"I went by there yesterday to check on my personal belongings that I have stored in that barn and someone tried to attack me."

"You mean rape you?"

"No, I don't think he wanted to do that. I think he was just trying to scare me away from there."

"Did he do that?"

"Yes, he sure did. I had to stay hidden on the mountain until dark before I could finally leave. I was scared he would kill me if he caught me."

"Did you see him?"

"No, I never did see his face. All I really did was hear him. Especially when he was chasing me."

"How did the barn become unlocked?"

"I unlocked it, but the guy started knocking my boxes over on me so I had to get out of there fast. I dropped the lock on the ground and took off running."

"Is anyone living there? I mean, besides you?"

"No, no one lives there. I don't live there yet, but I will. There shouldn't be anyone living or hiding on the property. The house, the old Thompson home place, burned down several months ago."

"Are you related to Jim Thompson?"

"Yes, he was my uncle."

"He sure was a strange one."

"Yeah, I know."

"I'll get on the radio and see if there are any officers in the area. You said Dry Branch?"

"It's near the Elk Mountain School. The road that runs past the school."

"Yes, I know where it is."

I could hear bursts of rapid speech filling the room from radio communications.

"How long will it take you to get to the property driving from here?"

"About fifteen or twenty minutes."

"Deputy Stevenson will meet you at the school in fifteen or twenty minutes and follow you to the property."

"Oh, thank you so much," I gushed as relief covered me like a blanket. I grabbed my car keys and headed for the door, "Thank you again, Deputy Martin. I really was afraid to go there by myself but if I had to do that, I would have."

I arrived at the school and there was no sheriff's car waiting. I sat in my car watching and wondering what had happened.

A half-hour later it became abundantly clear that the deputy was not going to make an appearance. I had no wireless telephone and there certainly wasn't any pay telephone around so I went on to the property alone.

Once again I parked at the top of the hill, but I was going to be prepared to fight if I met my trespasser again. I grabbed the tire iron out of the trunk of my car and held it up in front of me. I was prepared to strike at anyone who materialized before my eyes.

As I walked closer and closer to the barn, my nerves were tingling with fear and the need to do something.

I scolded myself for even thinking about doing something as stupid as the idea was in one breath. In the next breath I was rationalizing about why it was necessary to check the barn.

I didn't hear anything unusual. The birds were singing. The squirrels were chattering and chasing each other in the big apple tree in what used to be the front yard of the house. Some of the cattle had wandered down to the wagon path and were grazing on the sweet, tender grass in the area where Uncle Jim's garden used to be planted. Either someone or something had knocked the fence down allowing the cattle to graze in the garden or perhaps it had fallen down due to disrepair. The cattle seemed to be enjoying their unexpected tasty treat.

The actions of the animals and birds put me at ease a little. If there was something wrong, something out of the ordinary happening, they wouldn't be acting as if the day was ordinary. They would either be making a loud noisy fuss or they wouldn't be making any noise at all.

The feeling of ease didn't last very long.

When I was in front of the barn, I could see that the doors had been locked.

"Should I go inside?" I asked the wind as I walked closer to the locked barn doors.

I knew I had to check it out. I had to see if my stuff was still inside.

I pulled the key from my pocket and slipped it into the lock. The snap of the lock as it opened sounded loud enough to wake the dead.

I looked around.

I saw no one.

I heard nothing. Nothing, I heard nothing. Immediately my nerves tightened more. I knew I should be hearing the wild life. I should be hearing the cattle, the squirrels, the birds, but I heard no sounds at all except my own shallow breathing.

"Should I drop the lock again and run for the car? Should I take a stand and possibly get myself killed? Should I just jerk the doors open?" I asked as I reached for the doors.

That's exactly what I did. I knew it wasn't the smartest thing I could do, but I had to see. I had to take control of my life and not let some stranger try to scare me to death.

71

Once my eyes adjusted to the sudden darkness, I could see inside the barn. The boxes that had been knocked over onto me had been refilled of their spilled contents and restocked neatly onto the pile. Everything looked untouched.

"What's going on?" I asked in a whisper.

I walked around the pile of my belongings and saw nothing, or no one lurking in the barn.

I left the barn, locked it, and with the tire iron in my hand, I started walking up the hill to get back to my car.

The day was beautiful, the birds were singing, and the cattle were milling around munching on the greenery.

"Maybe it was just a homeless person passing through," I mumbled as I drove back to town.

I realized that I was talking to myself again.

I decided to make another stop at the sheriff's office. I wanted to know why Deputy Stevenson didn't show up.

"May I speak with Deputy Martin, please?"

"He's off duty, ma'am. I'm Deputy Jones. What can I do for you?"

"Deputy Martin told me Deputy Stevenson would meet me at my property on Dry Branch, but Deputy Stevenson didn't show up. Could you tell me why?"

"Let me check."

The deputy walked over to a desk and looked at a clipboard.

"What time was he supposed to meet you?"

"About an hour ago."

"He signed off sick about an hour ago. That's why I'm here."

"Thanks for nothing," I said as I walked out of the office filled with the feeling of disgust.

"I don't know what's going on in this town," I mumbled as I started my car, "but I'm going to find out."

CHAPTER 10
IS OHIO A FOREIGN COUNTRY?

Monday morning arrived with the promise of hope in finding some answers.

My first task for the day was to find a telephone book and a telephone I could use to call for installation of telephone and cable services. I had to drive all the way into Lebanon to find a pay telephone to use to make my calls. I made a note to myself that I needed to buy a cell phone.

I was in luck for once because I was told that both services could be up and running by late that afternoon. That was a tremendous help because the acquisition of my telephone would allow me to have a contact point when I submitted job applications. The purchase of the cell phone could wait.

I purchased a local newspaper from a convenience store I passed on my way home. I, also, purchased newspapers for Richlands, Stillwell, Bluefield, and Bristol. I couldn't find one for Abingdon or I would have picked one up for that city also.

My afternoon would be spent perusing the classified advertisements in each newspaper.

I had to find a job. I would be able to function on the money I had saved for a few weeks, but if I hadn't found a job by the time my money was spent, I didn't know what I would do.

I didn't want to travel great distances to work, but I would have to take what I could get no matter how far from home it took me.

The telephone installer and the cable installer both converged on my little trailer at the same time. My telephone was a necessity especially because I was job hunting. I also felt the cable television hookup was a necessity in order for me to maintain my sanity. I lived alone and I found I was talking to myself more and more just to hear a voice even if it was my own voice.

I was so happy to see both men that I would have gladly hugged them in gratitude if I thought they wouldn't misconstrue my actions. This was a small town, after all, and grown up, middle-aged women didn't go about hugging strange men. It just wasn't done.

"Oh, well, it's their loss," I thought as I controlled my need to hug.

It was after four o'clock when both men left my house. I turned on the television for the sake of having noise in the house.

I decided to wait until the next morning to call businesses for appointments for job applications. It was too late in the day and most employers wouldn't want to be bothered in my opinion.

Tuesday morning at nine o'clock I started making telephone calls to answer job advertisements in the local newspaper.

At several of the places I called, I was questioned about where I was calling from and how I came across the name of their business?

When I explained I was calling locally and that I found their business name in the local telephone book or local newspaper, I could feel the doubt crop up in their voices.

"Did I sound that different? I really didn't consider Ohio a foreign country but maybe I was wrong," I mused.

I had lived more than half of my life in northern Ohio, which had directed my speech patterns to take on the characteristics of a person from the north. A northerner was a person not to be trusted in Virginia. It appeared that the south was continuing to carry a grudge. At least, the southerners in southwest Virginia were carrying on the tradition.

I consciously tried to sound like a local but I couldn't.

It was apparent that I had been educated in the north, therefore I was a northerner. Never mind the fact that I was born in Charlottesville, Virginia.

After a couple of calls, I realized that the advertised jobs were snatched up right away by the locals and that I would have to do foot duty up and down Main Street.

I was going to go to every recognizable legitimate business and submit an application as a walk in off the street type of thing. I was afraid that was the only way I was going to beat the rush for the advertised jobs.

The first step would be to go into the businesses and ask for an application that I would take to the car for completing that evening.

If they had no printed application form available, I would leave a copy of my resumé with whomever I spoke and be on my way. I always received second looks when I spoke which clearly indicated that I was an unacceptable outsider.

After a couple of days of picking up and dropping off applications along with resumés, I decided to go the state funded employment service to seek help.

The slow economy and the depressed condition of the coal industry had the southwest end of Virginia in a squeeze. There were more people looking for jobs than there were jobs available.

I was going to have to search harder and accept less if I planned to survive. I knew the locals would get the first opportunity and the fact that I was an outsider was going to be a major disadvantage.

The employment office sent me to a bank to apply for a job as a file clerk for minimum wage.

The lady in the employment office told me that they hadn't sent very many people to apply for the job because it was only paying minimum wage.

"I'll take anything right now," I said excitedly. "It might lead to bigger and better things since it's in a bank."

The bank was in Richlands while I was living in Lebanon, but that didn't matter because I needed a job.

"I'm Charles Crown. You are?"

"Ellen Hutchins. The employment office gave me the address. I'm looking for a job."

"Where are you from?"

"Why? Is that a problem?"

"No, not a problem. You sound a little different from the local people."

"I've moved here from Ohio, but my family is from here, at least, my mother's side is from Richard County."

"From the looks of your application you have done a lot of different jobs. Your last job was for a steel company. You've also had training as a legal secretary?"

"Yes sir."

"Why do you want to work here?"

"I need a job that pays."

"It only pays minimum wage."

"I know, but I still need a job."

"Let me see," he said as he glanced at my application, "yes, there it is. I'll call you tomorrow after I discuss your application with a couple of people."

"Thank you, Mr. Crown, for speaking with me. I hope you call me."

I left with only a glimmer of hope sparkling in the distance. Perhaps my having been a legal secretary was a good thing? All I could do was hope.

I had no more job interviews that day and the prospects of getting any more interviews soon were getting slimmer with each passing hour.

I bought another weekly newspaper for Lebanon, Richlands, and Stillwell from the convenience store. I drove home to wait and worry as I gazed at the newspapers looking for something, anything I could get paid for doing. Even McDonald's sounded good. I truly was getting desperate.

Mr. Crown called the next day and told me I could start work the following morning. I was so excited I couldn't sleep.

CHAPTER 11
TOM WALKER, THE MAN OF MY DREAMS

A job! I had a job. I was well on my way to becoming a full-fledged productive member of the local economy and community.

Maybe I could call the place home soon, I hoped.

My job started out to be exactly what I was told it was. I was a file clerk except that I was trying to locate items within particular files. If they were not where they were supposed to be, I had to make a note of the missing item so I could look elsewhere at another time.

Boring was the descriptive word for what I was doing. I became very familiar with the files and was able to prove to Mr. Crown that I was capable of performing more difficult tasks that allowed me to gain his trust and more responsibility.

Eventually I was moved into the mortgage loan department. Mr. Crown was interested in getting into the mortgage selling end of banking.

"Ellen, in your experience as a legal secretary, did you do many loan closings for real estate?"

"Several times in Ohio. I haven't done any here in Virginia so I don't know what the laws and regulations are."

"I'm interested in your taking loan applications and doing the necessary and required paperwork to sell the mortgage loan after it has been completed to a mortgage broker. Do you think you can do that?"

"I don't know, Mr. Crown. I would have to see what's involved before I could answer that question."

"With this added responsibility you would be getting some more money. About a dollar more an hour at this time. Possibly more money down the road."

"That sounds great, Mr. Crown. When do you want me to start?"

"Tomorrow, I want you to start interviewing applicants tomorrow."

"I'll do the best I can," I said as Mr. Crown left the room.

"Wow, tomorrow! How was I going to learn everything I needed to know overnight?" I excitedly wondered.

I pulled the loan application information together and anything else I could think of that I might need to know and threw it into a box. I would carry that box home with me and learn as much as I could as fast as I could. I didn't want to make a complete fool out of myself the next day.

The bank attorney was Tom Walker and he would prove to be a fountain of information for me. We developed a really good telephone rapport that ultimately led to bigger and better things.

Tom and I were telephone friends until one day when he decided that we should meet face to face.

For weeks I had an image of him in my mind as an exceedingly handsome, outgoing man close to my own age, perhaps a little older. His voice projected a mental picture of his being self-confident and sure of himself with everything he tackled in life.

I wanted to meet Tom to see if he looked anything like I had pictured him in my mind. I didn't want him to meet me because I was so afraid he would be disappointed with my appearance. I was fat and lonely and I wasn't anything like the person I pretended to be when we were talking on the telephone.

"Ellen, I'm going to be stopping by the bank on Wednesday. I'll drop off the title searches I have completed rather than mailing them. Do you think you could go to lunch with me?"

"Sure, as long as I don't get roped into a mortgage interview. Sometimes I can't even go to lunch. I usually get bombarded by people who are on their lunch hour. Many people use that time to check out the mortgage rates, especially since the rates have dropped because the government is trying to bolster the economy."

"I hope you can go to lunch with me. I have something I want to talk to you about."

"Is it something you need me to do?"

"Yes, but it can wait until I talk to you on Wednesday. See you then."

"Okay," I said apprehensively as I hung up the telephone.

I couldn't imagine what he wanted to talk to me about that had to wait until Wednesday.

I really wanted to see Tom. I had wanted to know what kind of person he was. How old he was? What did he look like? But the description I received had been vague using such terms as average height, medium brown hair, late thirties or early forties, nice looking man. That could fit millions of males.

Wednesday morning arrived and I prayed to be busy. I wanted to have people lined up outside my door waiting to talk to me. I wanted to be too busy to go to lunch with Tom Walker, the man of my dreams.

I wanted my dreams to be just that – dreams. I didn't want to face reality nor did I want him to face the reality of the size sixteen Ellen. Considering the size twenty I had worn a couple of years earlier, my size sixteen body, even though it was beyond average, made me look svelte and sleek in comparison.

I was busy working at shuffling the mounds of paper I had accumulated on my desk when lunchtime arrived.

I had had no loan applicants that morning and it looked as if that would hold true for the afternoon. People were going about their business that day but it was not related to mortgage loans.

I heard a familiar voice coming from the lobby. I knew Tom Walker had arrived and that I would finally get to meet him face to face.

Mr. Crown must have garnered Tom's attention and taken him to his office for a private conversation. Tom's distinctive tones were no longer emanating from the lobby.

I was having a difficult time trying to force my mind to focus on the task at hand whatever it was as contained in the file folders in front of me. While my mind was wandering, Tom and Mr. Crown walked into my office.

I stood up quickly from my chair behind the desk as Tom and Mr. Crown proceeded to sit on the chairs in front of me.

"Ellen, you know Tom, don't you?"

"I've had numerous telephone conversations with Tom, but this is the first time we've actually met."

I held my hand forward for Tom to acknowledge with a handshake. Only then when I had my hand extended did I discover that he had only one functional hand. There was no hand extending from one of his sleeves.

Tom clasped my hand with his left hand shaking it firmly and sat down.

I struggled to close my mouth after I discovered the awkwardness of the situation. I was so embarrassed. Shame had reddened my face and made me feel warm, too warm for comfort.

"Tom, it's so nice to finally meet you. We've had some really good telephone conversations," I said as I tried to use the kind words to pull me from the pit of embarrassment.

"Mr. Crown, Ellen has been really quick with learning all of the legal ins and outs of the requirements for the loan closings. She makes my job a whole lot easier and a lot less costly for the bank, you know."

I was feeling the heat of embarrassment again except it was good, pleasant heat, not the ugly, shame from not knowing that Tom had an obvious disability.

"Why had no one told me?" I puzzled in my overactive mind.

Mr. Crown was called away by a telephone call. He left Tom sitting in my office and I was glad to see the moment come.

"Ellen, are you still going to lunch with me?"

"You still want me to go?"

"Sure, why wouldn't I?"

"No reason. I thought maybe Mr. Crown had roped you into joining him for lunch."

"Oh, he tried but I told him I already had plans. He won't get upset if we walk out together, will he?"

"Probably, but that's okay. He needs to know he's not always first choice, doesn't he?"

"Let's go, Ellen."

I grabbed my handbag and Tom Walker escorted me out through the lobby and out the front door of the bank with the heads of my coworkers turning as they followed Tom and me through the lobby with their eyes.

It sure did feel good to be noticed. I felt so proud as Tom and I walked out the front door to go to lunch.

Tom and I would be the subject of several whispered conversations. The thought of all the speculation and guessing made me want to giggle out loud.

Once again, I could feel the heat rising up inside me, but this time it was so different from the other times. This time I wasn't embarrassed.

CHAPTER 12
MY FIRST DATE

"Where do you want to go eat?"

"How about Shoney's?"

"Sounds good."

Tom drove as I sat across from him on the front seat of the car.

"You won't get into trouble if lunch takes a little longer than an hour, will you?" he asked as he smiled at me.

"No, I shouldn't. The bank owes me many lunch hours that I've never taken. I know Shoney's has a reputation for slow service, but I didn't think its reputation had reached all the way to Stillwell."

Tom smiled again upon hearing my remark. The glint in his eye showed me that he had an agenda and that it was his secret until he was ready to share it with me.

The restaurant lived up to its well-deserved reputation of being slow. Despite the slowness, we were finished with their lunch and ready to leave in an hour.

While we were sitting in the car, Tom finally got around to his real reason for asking me to lunch.

"Ellen, would you like to go to a movie this weekend?" he asked shyly.

"Sure," was all I could say.

"You told me before that you live in Lebanon. You need to give me directions to your house."

"Okay," again my response was short and sweet.

"What kind of movies do you like?"

"You want to drive all the way from Stillwell to pick me up to go to a movie?"

"Of course, I do."

"What movie theatre do you want to go to?"

"Depends on what you want to see."

"I haven't been to a movie in a long time. I've never been to a movie since moving here. All of the movies out now are new to me. You pick one out."

"Okay, we'll go to a movie in Bluefield."

"You want to drive from Stillwell to Lebanon which is about thirty miles, give or take a couple of miles, pick me up, then turn around and retrace those thirty miles, and drive another twenty miles so we can go to a movie?"

"We could go see one in Abingdon?"

"That's about the same amount of driving except that's it's in the opposite direction."

"I know, Ellen, but we don't have much of a choice. We live in the middle of nowhere."

"We don't have to go to a movie. I could rent a couple of movies and you could come to The Ellen Hutchins Drive-In Theatre."

"That's not much of a first date, Ellen."

"Well, we could go eat first then rent the movie. How's that?"

"That's good for me. If you don't mind?"

"I wouldn't have suggested it if I minded."

He drove me back to work and dropped me off at the front door of the bank after I told him I would fax the directions to my home and telephone number to him at his office that same afternoon.

I walked into the bank with a smile glued to my face. No matter how hard I tried, I could not turn off the smile.

It really felt great to be accepted in a new world that was so different from the one I had left.

The fact that I was different, maybe that was the reason Tom was attracted to me. I knew I was a little standoffish, as my mother would have said. My mother would have known because my dad was the same way, which annoyed my mother to no end.

Having lived in a big city, I had learned to trust no one. I feared that ability would not change. I didn't know if I really wanted it to change.

If you wanted bubbles and a glowing personality, knocking on my front door wasn't going to get you what you wanted.

If you wanted truth and sincerity, I could provide that image with just a touch of humor.

I envied those bubbly, happy all the time people but I knew I didn't have the ingredients to be that way. I had tried all of my life to be what I wasn't. In my forties, I finally accepted myself, so those around me would have to do the same or seek friendship elsewhere.

I wasn't trying to be a hard-nose about my nature. I fervently hoped Tom realized that the happy-go-lucky person I presented to him over the telephone was my form of inviting him into my life. I had to work at being happy-go-lucky and I would do it again and again to flag his interest.

I liked Tom. I liked our telephone conversations. I liked our lunch. I liked everything about him.

I hoped he felt the same way.

I knew the rest of the work-week would pass slowly as I anxiously awaited my date with Tom.

I hadn't been able to do much snooping into the life and times of Uncle Jim.

After work on Thursday, I decided I would drive to the property and check the barn. It was still early evening when I reached Dry Fork. I had tried to put my previous frightening experience out of my mind, but I couldn't. I constantly glanced over my shoulder to see if anyone was

85

behind me and I strained my eyes as I checked out everything in front of me as I walked from the top of the hill down to the ashes of the old home place.

I was drawn to those ashes each time I visited the land and barn. My heritage was destroyed in those ashes. My ancestral history and the faces of my family in the form of photographs were destroyed forever.

I picked up a stick and started poking at the ashes again and again.

Was I hoping that the truth would rise up out of those ashes? Maybe.

Did I really think the ghosts of my ancestors would rattle their chains and lead me to the answer as to why and how Uncle Jim was killed? I could only hope.

I was so focused on those ashes and their hidden secrets that I didn't hear the man approaching me from behind my back.

Suddenly I felt his presence.

Fear flowed through me and my flight or fight mechanism in my brain went into gear and immediately chose flight.

I took off running as fast as my short, chubby legs could carry me. I couldn't look back. It would take too much time.

My only hope of escape was to get to my cousin's house. Maybe my cousin could help me.

I climbed and scrambled up the hill that was behind what used to be the house and now was only ashes.

I wanted to turn and shove my chaser down the hill.

I wanted to twist his arm and cause him so much pain that he would tell me what was going on, why this was happening to me.

Most of all, I wanted him to tell me who he was.

My shoes were running shoes and they gripped the earth beneath the grass so that I wouldn't lose my balance and slide backward into the waiting arms of my chaser.

I pulled at the grass as I climbed willing the tufts of greenery to pull me up the hill faster and away from what I felt was certain death.

"Please, go away. Leave me alone," I whispered to myself. I was so breathless and scared that I could force my voice to go no louder.

"Why are you doing this?"

I heard no words from the body chasing me. I heard heavy breathing and grunts as he tried to follow me up the hill.

Then, I heard nothing.

I realized that I had climbed into the line of vision of anyone who might be inside the house standing at any of the windows facing the front of the house.

There was no car parked in front of the house but it could have been in the garage.

My chaser didn't know that there was no one at home. There was no one inside the house that could see him as he tried to dispose of me.

I turned around to see a figure clad in blue jeans and a work shirt running away from me towards the hill on the other side.

At the top of the hill, I saw a red SUV.

I continued to climb the hill until I reached the front yard of my cousin's house. I walked around to the back of my cousin's house and hid until I saw the red SUV leave.

I wanted the man chasing me to think I had entered the house and was getting help from my cousin.

I continued on with my quest to check on my belongings that were stored in the barn.

Everything appeared to be untouched.

I locked the barn and climbed the hill to get out of there. I didn't know how much more of this abuse I was going to be able to withstand.

Saturday arrived.

It was the night of my date.

I climbed out of bed very early because I was too excited to sleep. That seemed so silly to me. A woman in her forties excited about a date. You would have thought it was my first date, ever. In a way it was. It was my first date in my new life and I was as excited as a sixteen-year-old girl was.

I had the small trailer spotless and shining by ten o'clock. There were several hours of waiting before Tom would arrive to pick me up for dinner.

I decided it was high time that I went to visit a long lost cousin. That was a strange phrase coming from me.

My childhood brought with it very few memories of extended family relationships. My mom and dad had been married thirty-nine years when my dad died on the date of their thirty-ninth anniversary. That says a lot for the longevity of their relationship, but my mother was actually my dad's second wife. My mother had only been married once and that was to my father.

My father had four children by his first wife and it seemed the extended family- meaning aunts, uncles, and cousins- did not welcome my mother into the family fold willingly. My mother's family did not welcome my dad into their branch of the family tree openly because he had been married prior to marrying my mother.

As a result of the feeling of being unaccepted on both sides of the family, my mother visited her mother every other year and my father visited his mother and father every other year. The only other contact that was had was by mail until telephones became a common instrument of communication.

The telephone brought with it the ability for my oldest half-brother, Francis, every time he got drunk, to call my father. In his drunken stupor, Francis would rehash all of the faults he ever saw in my father.

Many times I saw my father hang up the telephone as he forced back angry, bitter tears after listening to Francis rant and rave for several minutes.

I really didn't know everything about my father and his first wife. I never met her nor did I ever want to do so.

Life before my mother, my brother, and myself must have been hard for my father to bear. As I had been told, my father wanted to do whatever it would take to keep his family of a wife and four children together.

It appeared that his wife, Aletha, didn't feel the same way. My father caught her out with another man. When he did so, he filed for divorce and it was granted.

They began seeing each other again and Aletha promised to be faithful so they remarried for the sake of the children.

One day when my father arrived home early, unexpectedly, from work, he found Aletha in his bed with another man.

My father, once again, filed for divorce and, once again, it was granted.

"If my dad was so wrong, as Francis had told him time and time again, how come the divorces were granted so easily even with children involved in the state of Virginia where a divorce was so hard to get?" was a question I only voiced in my mind.

That Francis would squarely place the blame on my father didn't set well with me at all. Many times I wanted to reach through that telephone and wrap the cord around my half-brother's neck. But, I didn't say anything because I had no right to get involved in a relationship that was formed long before I was conceived. I loved my father and I knew he didn't want my pity. He wanted only my understanding and love.

The extended family on my father's side looked at me and my brother as outsiders only to be tolerated.

The extended family on my mother's side looked at my father as not good enough for my mother; therefore, Lee and I, his offspring, were not good enough.

I often envied people with large families who appeared to like each other. They always had each other to depend on in times of need.

I never had that feeling of dependence and closeness. Would I have loved that feeling? I didn't know but it would have been nice to find out before it was too late.

The cousin who lived on the hill above the house my Uncle Jim lived in was younger than I was. I couldn't remember why I was her cousin. My family tree had never been mapped out for me to see from which branch she fell.

I didn't particularly care that she was family. My only interest in my cousin was to find out if she knew anything about Uncle Jim's death, about his friends, and about his way of life.

My cousin might have possibly known the killer.

My cousin could have been the killer.

CHAPTER 13
COUSIN MAGGIE

Cousin Maggie, who lived on top of the hill, was not at all friendly. That didn't surprise me. After all, I was an obvious outsider.

"Maggie, isn't it?" I asked Margaret Fox after she opened her front door a sliver.

"Yes?"

"I'm Ellen Hutchins. Jim Thompson was my uncle. Could I talk to you for a few minutes?"

"What about?" she asked abruptly.

"About Uncle Jim. I'm trying to find out as much about him as I can."

"Why? He was your uncle, not your father?"

"He was my uncle who was murdered by someone who hasn't been made to pay for his crime. I'd like to know who that someone is. Wouldn't you?"

Maggie looked down at my feet then followed my body up to my face with her critical eyes. She pushed the door closed. I heard a chain rattling as she slid it over so she could open the door completely. She motioned for me to enter and pointed to a chair in her living room.

Before me I saw a young woman, in her thirties perhaps, who had the harried, rushed appearance of someone who didn't want to be bothered. My cousin's brown hair was tousled and her brow was etched with lines of irritation.

"I don't know anything."

"How long have you lived here?"

"Since my grandmother died. She left the house to me along with some money to fix it up."

"How long ago was that?"

"About five years."

"Then you've been here long enough to have known Uncle Jim."

"You didn't know your Uncle Jim. He wouldn't let anyone visit him without a fight. That's the way he treated most everyone."

"You were family. Why didn't he let you visit?"

"I don't have any idea. He was a crazy old coot always shooting off his gun. I had to call the law on him a couple of times," Maggie said angrily as the tone of her voice was taking on a louder, harsher sound.

"How come?"

"He kept shooting that gun of his. He claimed he was killing groundhogs and rats."

"Was he?"

"I never saw any animal carcasses. Anyway, after the first blast from that gun any wild animal living around him would have been long gone. But, he kept shooting. Every few minutes you would hear his gun go off. I was afraid to walk out the door. I didn't know which direction he was shooting. So I called the sheriff for help."

"I don't blame you for that. What did the sheriff say? Was that Sheriff Dunsmore?"

"Said he was killing groundhogs and rats like I already told you. Sheriff Dunsmore didn't come any of the times I called. He sent a deputy, Stevenson was his name, I think. I think he was the son of one of the guys that your uncle went to high school with that came when I called. He wasn't going to do anything to his daddy's buddy, your uncle, and, of course, the deputy would believe what Jim told him. Jim and his daddy were buddies. Jim wouldn't lie to him is what he told me."

"Why do you think he was shooting the gun?"

"I don't know but he wasn't killing groundhogs or rats, not after the first shot. That's all I know."

"Did you ever see a woman go to Uncle Jim's house?"

"No, never, unless she was a relative like you or your mother. I've seen you two there. I've seen Pat and her kids there, but that's all. There was no other woman."

"What about men? Did he have any man friends?"

"Not many. I saw a couple of men at different times park at the top of the hill and walk down to his house. If they park at the top, I can see their cars when I look out my front door. I have to pass the parked cars when I come home from work. He's had company a few times but not many."

"Do you know who they were? The men, I mean."

"I didn't get a close enough look. I've seen the cars in town though. I know they're from around here."

"Did anybody else visit?"

"You certainly are nosey for a niece, a not well-liked niece, at that."

"How would you know if I was not well-liked?" I asked as my temper was starting to respond to my cousin's words.

"I've just heard rumors. They say that Jim didn't like your family at all. Except his sister, he liked her."

"I didn't like him very much either, but he was murdered. No one has a right to murder someone else, do they?"

"I guess not."

"Like I asked before, did anyone else visit Uncle Jim?"

"The teenage boys."

"What teenage boys? Who were they?"

"I don't know who they were. They didn't look like they belonged around here."

"Why? What was so different about them?"

"They were dirty, rough looking. They might have been runaways. I was afraid they would come here and take everything I owned. That's why I had the chain put on the door. I was afraid of them."

"Did they ever do anything to you?"

"No, but I wasn't going to give them a chance to."

"How many of them were there?"

"Sometimes only one. Other times there would be three or four there."

"And you didn't know any of them?"

"No, I'd never seen them before they started showing up around here."

"Did you tell the sheriff about the boys?"

"Yes, but he wasn't as interested as you are?"

"The day they said he was killed, were you home?"

"No, I was at work."

"What about the day before?"

"What about it?"

"Did you see anything? Hear anything?"

"I can't really answer that. I don't know what day he was killed. Do you?"

"No, I guess not."

"I've got things to do. I work during the week so I do my grocery shopping and everything else on the weekend. If you have finished with your questions, I would like to get on with my chores."

"Oh, sure. I'm sorry about holding you up. Can I have your telephone number in case I have any other questions?"

Maggie wrote the number down on a piece of paper that I handed her along with a pen. I wrote my telephone number on a separate piece of paper and gave it to my cousin.

"Call me if you think of anything else that might help. Anything that you remember, however small the detail, might help pin the killer down so we can find out who it is."

I walked out of the house with the feeling that Cousin Maggie knew something else.

"Did Cousin Maggie kill Uncle Jim?"

I didn't think so, but I'd been wrong before.

I turned around quickly and headed back to my cousin's front door. Maggie must have seen me coming because she opened the door as soon as I stepped on to the porch.

"I forgot to ask you about the cars you saw parked at the top of the hill," I said as I fought to regain control of my rapid breathing.

"What about them?"

"What kind of cars were they? Ford? Chevrolet? What?"

"They were SUV's, you know, those big old truck-sized station wagons, those go anywhere, do anything, almost truck vehicles."

"Why on earth would they park that kind of vehicle at the top of the hill? Those vehicles would have made it down the hill without any problem."

"You would think that, wouldn't you? Maybe they were trying to surprise him."

"Maybe. You can't see the cars parked at the top of the hill from inside the house. I don't think you can see them from anywhere near the house if they are parked back from the edge of hill."

"When Uncle Jim was shooting his gun, you think he might have been trying to discourage visitors?"

"Could have been. Could have been some kind of warning or maybe a threat."

"What color were the vehicles?"

"One was maroon, you know, a dark purplish red. Another was silver gray. I think there was a third one that was black."

"Were they all parked there at the same time?"

"No. I only saw one at a time."

"You didn't recognize anybody?"

"I told you no. They were too far away."

"You didn't get a license number, did you?"

"I did once because the vehicle was blocking my road. I just barely had enough space to get by that vehicle without rolling or sliding down the hill. I was going to call the sheriff if it happened again."

"Did it happen again?"

"No and I threw the license number away just in case you wanted to ask me to show it to you. Now, if you don't mind?"

"Thanks, Maggie. Thanks for all of your help. No one's been willing to talk to me very much about what happened."

"I didn't tell you anything that isn't on file in the sheriff's office," she said as she closed the door again.

I took the sudden appearance of the door directly in front of me as my signal to leave. Cousin Maggie was tired of me and my questions.

I walked to my car but before I climbed inside of it, I walked to the edge of the hillside where it started sharply sloping down to the backside of where Uncle Jim's house used to stand.

Maggie was right about not being able to see anything going on at Uncle Jim's house. You had to walk to the very edge of the steep slope to see the back porch of the house that stood at the bottom of the hill.

It really was an awfully lonely place.

CHAPTER 14
MAKING OUR OWN MOVIE

I drove back to the trailer with my head filled with many more questions for which I had no answers.

I had purchased a tape recorder for some unknown reason in my boring past. That tape recorder was going to be the place for me to store my information gathered, the answers to my questions, and my theories.

I tried to repeat everything I had been told by Maggie into the small machine. Then I added some descriptive detail about Cousin Maggie's appearance, her attitude, and the feeling that I had when I left her home.

I then took the tiny recorded tape and hid it in the breaker box that directed the power to various parts of the trailer. I inserted the recorded tape into a sandwich bag that I folded as small as possible and taped bag and recorded tape with duct tape to the inside of the door covering the box.

With the kind of reception I had been experiencing when I asked questions about Uncle Jim, I thought it was better to be safe than sorry.

I made myself a peanut butter sandwich and watched television to help pass the time until Tom picked me up for our dinner date.

I heard or saw very few cars pass the front of the trailer. The trailer was also an awfully lonely place especially when you're a wee bit scared. I knew that if I continued to think about everything that had been happening to me and to Uncle Jim, I would become too scared to continue probing into the problem.

I had to focus my mind on something else. That wasn't hard to do because Tom immediately filled every crack and crevice of my mind when I pushed Uncle Jim away from the front of my brain.

All of the conversations we had had by telephone ostensibly for bank business had been humorously seductive and outrageously flirtatious at both ends of the conversation. I truly never dreamed that I would be dating the man that I would have laid down for twenty or thirty times on the telephone.

It was funny to see us both struggle for the right words to say to each other when we went to lunch. I hoped that uneasy, unspoken feeling would disappear.

I didn't want to jump his bones that night and I didn't want him to think that I did. I also didn't want him to think that the purpose of watching a movie in my living room was because of its close proximity to my bed. I wanted to be courted and respected. In time, I wanted to be loved if that happened to fit into the picture.

I didn't know what to wear. Maybe a dress? No, that would be too dressy. Something that I normally would wear to work accented with a piece of jewelry.

Maybe a pair of slacks and a blazer with a dressy, sophisticated blouse peeking through to draw the eye away from the pants.

A skirt and sparkly blouse? No, that would be too much.

I decided the navy slacks with a blazer and a nicely feminine blouse would be appropriate. I was sure we weren't going to go eat anywhere that there might be a need to dress formal. At least, I knew of no place like that in and around Lebanon.

He had told me he would be at the trailer at six and at precisely six o'clock he was knocking on my door.

"Come on in, Tom. I'll show you my wonderful, newly rented home," I said with an embarrassed smile.

It hadn't occurred to me that the appearance of the tiny trailer might be a source of embarrassment until I opened the door to admit my date. Tom had to bend his neck to get his head low enough so that he wouldn't hit his head on the doorframe. When I saw him duck, a bit of a nervous giggle escaped from my mouth.

"Geez, Tom, I didn't realize you were too tall for the trailer," I said with a laugh.

"I'm too tall for some of the houses that are built in southwestern Virginia. It seems that the men of days gone by were built much closer to the ground which is how they built their houses. Don't worry about it, Ellen. It happens," he said with a smile that melted my heart.

"I'm planning to buy a double-wide and move it onto the property I inherited from my Uncle Jim as soon as my money allows me to do that."

"Where is that?"

"That's a long story, Tom. Maybe we can talk about it later. Right now, I'm starved. Where are we going to eat?"

"How about the Steak House?"

"That's great. That's my kind of food, Tom. I'm basically a meat and potatoes person."

We walked to the car where Tom opened my door and extended his hand to offer assistance. I had never, ever had anybody do that. I was impressed.

He walked around the back of the car and climbed onto the front seat. He turned towards me.

"Ellen, I wish I didn't have bucket seats in this car. What I wouldn't give for a bench seat right now so I could ask you to move here. Close to me."

I looked at him and smiled. I had been thinking the same thing. I hoped the smile washed away the blush.

The Steak House was in downtown Lebanon. The drive was going to be short so we decided to rent the movie and leave it in the car waiting for us to finish our dinner.

When we were seated inside the restaurant, we both were silent, searching for words.

"We didn't have trouble talking to each other on the telephone, did we?" I said with a timid laugh.

"No, but now that we are face to face, I'm afraid I'll say something that might offend you."

"Let's get back to the way we were. You know I don't offend easily or you wouldn't have been comfortable talking to me like you did on the telephone. I know you don't offend easily or you would have let your feelings be known in the tone of your conversations with me. Am I right?"

He nodded and we both smiled.

"What brought you to Virginia, especially to this area, Ellen?"

"I get asked that question quite often. I've given up trying to figure out why that is always a topic of any and all conversations with me."

"You're different, Ellen. People are just curious as to why you would choose this area of the country."

"Are you trying to ask me 'what is a nice girl like me doing in a place like this?" I asked with a smile.

"I sure am. Why are you here? You weren't born in Virginia. You sound northern."

"Well, you're wrong, Tom. I was born in Virginia. I was born in Charlottesville. My mom's family is from Richard County. That's where she was born."

"How come you don't sound like a Virginian?"

"Because I've spent most of my life in Ohio. That's where my dad's job led him. I have roots in this area because of my mother. I was just looking for a place to live out my life in peace away from the rat race that a big city has to offer."

"Have you found that peace?"

"Not yet. I don't think I will until I get a few questions answered about my uncle's death."

"Who was your uncle?"

"Jim Thompson was my uncle. He lived on some property on Dry Branch. Someone shot him and then burned the old home place down to the ground. So, as you can see, I haven't found any peace yet?"

"Who killed him?"

"I wish I knew."

"They don't know who did it?"

"No, if they do, they aren't telling me. I don't think they really care."

"Why would you say that?"

"Uncle Jim was not an ordinary, run-of-the-mill type of person. He was a loner, a recluse, who didn't want to see anybody at any time. That's what people told me. We, as family, didn't see him that way."

"How did you see him?'

"Do you really want to hear all of this?"

"Yes, sure."

"I always thought, no, I take that back. After I got old enough to understand what it meant, I thought my Uncle Jim was gay. Except for his mother, my grandmother, he had no contact with females on a daily basis whatsoever. If he wasn't gay, he sure built up a huge distrust for women."

"I'm sure the death was investigated. What did the sheriff have to say about it?"

"He thinks Uncle Jim was killed by a woman who robbed him."

"Don't you believe that?"

"No, I don't. First of all, I don't think there ever was a woman involved. Secondly, if there was a woman, no one ever saw her."

"It doesn't sound logical, does it?"

"No, it makes no sense at all."

"You are inheriting the property?"

"Yes, me and my brother. I don't think my Aunt Patti's children are involved because I was told Aunt Patti signed over her rights to the land to Uncle Jim. Mom never did that. My dad told her not to in case my brother or I wanted to come here to live. It's funny how that has worked out. I am here and I thought I never would move back to Virginia."

"I'm sure glad you did, Ellen," said Tom as he reached across the table to hold my hand.

"I want to try to borrow some money against the land so I can live on it. I'll need to hire a lawyer to search the title. Who would you recommend?"

"Me. I'll do it if you're not in a great hurry."

"I can't ask you to do that."

"You didn't. I volunteered and I mean I volunteered. No lawyer fees involved."

"No, Tom. I'd have to pay you."

"Okay, if you have to pay me, you can pay for any court fees I have to fork out for copies and such."

"That's the least I can do."

"Don't worry about it, Ellen. I want to know what happened to your Uncle Jim, too."

I didn't know what to say. Most everyone else I had approached or merely mentioned my uncle's death to brushed me off like a piece of lint. Tom, on the other hand, was ready to jump into the mess and start stirring the pot with a stick.

"Let's go watch the movie," suggested Tom as he picked up the bill.

The short drive to my trailer was refreshing. When he pulled into the driveway he turned off the headlights and reached for me. He gently pulled me over to him and kissed me. It was such a warm and wonderful kiss.

"Maybe I shouldn't go inside," said Tom when he released me from the kiss.

"Maybe you should," I answered as I leaned toward him to offer him welcome to my life, my heart, and my love.

We went inside and went through the motions of setting up the VCR, inserting the movie, and pressing the play button.

From the moment play was pressed, we were making our own movie.

I was in love. I was being loved. I was giving love. That covers about everything I was feeling at the time.

It wasn't an overnight happening. This feeling had been building up and up with our conversations over the telephone. I felt I knew Tom.

We may have been awkward and shy when we first met face to face but that passed. We discovered in each other what had attracted us in the first place.

The warm soft kisses led to exploring with gentle caresses and rapid heartbeats.

The sofa was not comfortable and the feelings were too intense not to let nature run its course.

Tom stayed with me the entire night and he loved me until we both fell away from each other due to exhaustion.

Even though my evening had started out with my feelings of being a teenager on my first date, the evening ended with the feelings that only two fulfilled, satisfied, loving adults could share.

I laid on the bed beside the man of my dreams and thought about how lucky I was to have this man beside me.

I picked my head up off the pillow so I could look at him. The light was not shining brightly in the bedroom so all I had to illuminate his presence was a nightlight that was putting forth its best effort in the bathroom.

I watched the rise and fall of his chest as he slept peacefully.

I wanted to touch him so that I would know he was really, really there.

I wanted to feel his warm skin beneath my head as I used him for a pillow.

I wanted to follow the outline of his mouth with my fingertips and then cover him with kisses until I fell into a dream filled, love filled sleep.

I didn't touch him.

I didn't wake him.

I let him sleep his peaceful sleep.

I finally lowered my head to my pillow and followed him to dream land where I continued to see and feel all the love he had to give.

CHAPTER 15
I CAN FIGHT DIRTY, TOO

After Tom left me on Sunday morning, I, once again, faced the world alone. It felt so good to have Tom by my side sharing my fears and doubts. Those fears and doubts returned rapidly after I watched Tom drive away to be swallowed by the brilliance of the rising morning sun.

"Was this only a one night stand? Would he want to come back to my arms to receive the love I have to offer? Would this cost me dearly in the form of heartbreak and pain? Would he ever call me again? Would he want to share his life with me again for a mere moment or a long, lingering, and loving evening?" I worried.

I didn't want to think about all of the things that could go wrong between Tom and me anymore.

I wanted only to remember how wonderful we felt.

I wanted to remember forever the love.

I was reveling in the beauty of remembrance when I was jarred back to reality by a knock on my door.

I jumped up immediately thinking it was Tom returning to me and my love.

I jerked the door open and was greatly disappointed.

"Sheriff Dunsmore, what can I do for you?"

"I thought I'd stop by and see how things are going. One of my deputies told me you had a problem a couple of months ago. Have you had any more problems?"

"None that require your attention. Since no one showed up the last time I asked for help, I wasn't planning to ask your office for help again if I could avoid it."

"I'm awful sorry about that mix up. Deputy Jones said one of my deputies was supposed to meet you at your uncle's place and the deputy didn't show up. Is that right?"

"Deputy Stevenson was supposed to meet me."

"I asked Deputy Stevenson about why he didn't meet you and he told me he never received the dispatch.'

"That's strange. The other deputy, Deputy Martin I think was his name, told me he had spoken to Deputy Stevenson. I heard part of the conversation on the radio. At least, I heard Deputy Martin's end of it clearly. The part received over the radio was garbled to me."

"There must have been a crossed up transmission somewhere because at the time Deputy Martin supposedly spoke with Deputy Stevenson, Deputy Stevenson was out of his car being sick. He said he never received the dispatch."

"Someone received it."

"Yes, but we don't know who it was."

"I find that hard to believe. Your deputy couldn't tell from the voice who he was talking to?"

"No, the transmission was garbled, like you said. He did hear an affirmative answer. Perhaps it wasn't the answer to the dispatch to help you. It may have been meant for someone else."

I nodded my head in acceptance. I didn't believe a word of it but what could I do? Call him a liar? Where was that going to get me any help when I needed it?

"Is that all you wanted, Sheriff?"

"Yes, I wanted to let you know that it won't happen again. Also, I wanted you to tell me what happened on the property that caused you to ask for help."

"Someone chased me all over the place. I thought he was trying to kill me. For the life of me, I couldn't figure out why? Do you have any ideas, Sheriff?"

"Did you see his face?"

"No, I didn't see him at all. I heard him and felt his presence."

"You probably just ran up on a bum, some old drunk, with no place to go."

"Maybe."

"I was going to stop by earlier but you had company."

"Yes, I did," I was confused at this point. I was wondering if my house was being watched.

"He had vanity plates that indicated he was a lawyer. Could I ask you who he was?"

"What made you think it was a he? Oh, forget that. I know you didn't need to ask me. You know who was here because you ran the plates through your computer."

"Yes, I did check them. I didn't want you to have any more problems since you're new to the area."

"Oh, really," was my sarcastic response.

"Are you in need of the services of an attorney? If you are, I could recommend a couple of locals. You wouldn't need one from Stillwell."

"No, Sheriff, I don't need a lawyer; not yet, anyway."

"Ellen, I'm going to get out of here. It's good to see you again. I hope you don't have any more problems," said Sheriff Dunsmore as he turned toward the door.

"Thanks, Sheriff. I hope I don't need you or your services again either."

I watched the sheriff get into his car, start the engine, and back out of the driveway.

He was trying to pry information out of me and he didn't do a very good job. This sneaky, underhanded business of watching me, checking on my visitors, and boldly knocking on my door was getting on my nerves.

"What's going on?" I wondered as I tried to rationalize everything into an acceptable form. "None of this makes sense," was all my mind would accept.

My fears of Tom Walker being a one night stand dissipated later that day when my telephone rang and he was cheerfully telling me what our next date would be like.

"Tom, do you have any enemies in Richard County?"

"None that I'm aware of. Why do you ask?"

"For some reason known only to God and Sheriff Dunsmore, he has been keeping tabs on me. He is or he's got someone watching my house. He saw your car and ran the plates so he knows you were visiting me."

"I haven't robbed any banks or killed anyone recently so there shouldn't be a problem," he said as he laughed loudly.

"You might not think it's funny when I tell you that the sheriff wanted to recommend a couple of other lawyers if I required any legal services."

"You're kidding."

"Nope, I'm not kidding. I don't know what's going on around here but I think I've gotten you involved. How do you feel about that, Tom? It wasn't intended, honestly."

"Bring'em on, Ellen. I can fight dirty, too, as long as I know who and why I'm fighting."

"My uncle's death and my getting his property is all I can think of that would be of interest to anybody where I'm concerned."

"I think you're right about that."

"I guess I've been asking too many questions even though I really haven't talked to very many people at all. Maybe I'm a threat because I moved here where I can see what's happening. They can't lie to me long distance anymore."

"You could be right about that, too."

"When can we see each other again?" I asked as I closed my eyes so I could see him in my mind.

"Is Wednesday all right?"

"Sure. I wish it were sooner. I have to wait three whole days," I said sadly trying to make it seem like a joke.

"I know but I have to go to Richmond tomorrow morning early and I won't be back until Wednesday afternoon."

"I understand but I'll miss you."

Our conversation lingered on as neither of us wanted to end that small point of contact.

Monday was a new day filled with the promise of the arrival of Wednesday.

Work was routine and tended to be boring at times so I decided to spice it up with a couple of telephone calls.

I remembered Uncle Jim talking about a friend of his who worked with him as the custodian at the local community college. After a few moments of struggling with my recall, I came up with the name of Sam Jenkins.

I checked the telephone white pages and garnered a number for S. Jenkins at Belfast.

"Mr. Jenkins?"

"Yes, can I help you?" asked a shaky, elderly voice.

"My name is Ellen Hutchins. I am or was Jim Thompson's niece. Would I be able to come to your house to talk to you about my Uncle Jim?"

"Why would you want to do that?" he asked with suspicion tingeing his voice.

"I've moved to Virginia from Ohio since Uncle Jim's death and I just wanted to talk to some of his friends. That's all."

"I don't know..."

"If it's an imposition, I won't do it."

"It's not that. When do you want to come by?"

"How about this evening about six o'clock, if that's okay?"

"Okay, I guess."

"I need directions to your house, Mr. Jenkins."

He explained the way to get to his house. The directions were complicated and I hoped I would get there on time. His directions would take me from the interstate to a paved county road to a couple of gravel roads. He didn't live on a well-traveled path.

I called Preacher Johnson to see what was happening. Just my way of being nosey, I guessed.

"Preacher Johnson, Al, this is Ellen Hutchins. I wanted to touch base with you and thank you again for helping me find a place to live."

"That was my pleasure, Ellen. How are things going with you?"

"Fine, Al. I've found a job in Richlands working in a bank."

"That's what I heard. Not much goes on around here without it being talked about, you know."

"That's small town life, isn't it, Al?"

"It sure is. Have you learned anything new about your uncle's death?"

I paused for a moment. I thought I was the one trying to pry some information from Preacher Johnson, but I thought now the roles were reversed.

"Ellen?"

"No sir. I really haven't discovered anything new at all."

"Neither have I. The rumor mill has been sort of quiet concerning your uncle. I guess that's good, isn't it?"

"Yeah, I suppose."

"Ellen, why don't you come to church on Sunday? We would love to have you there. I'll introduce you to the congregation."

"I'll think about it, Al. I haven't started into a church yet. Maybe it's time I did."

"In small towns, people talk; especially about single women who have male overnight visitors, if you know what I mean?"

"I wonder, Preacher Johnson, if everyone in this town is aware of how many times I flush my toilet?" I said angrily as I slammed down the telephone.

Tears were sparkling in my eyes, which always happened when I was angry. It was my defense mechanism, one that I truly hated. When I was angry, truly angry, I cried. There was nothing I could do to change that reaction. I had tried many times in my life.

Crying could be read in different ways. Many people cry when they're happy. Many cry when they are sad. I cried when I was mad. Boy did I hate that. I knew people misunderstood the meaning of my tears.

"These people need to get a life," I thought angrily as I made myself return to the paperwork spread out on my desk in front of me.

CHAPTER 16
TALKING TO SAM JENKINS

As I climbed into my car after finishing up my workday, I hoped dealing with Mr. Sam Jenkins would be better than my encounter with Preacher Johnson.

I had anticipated the drive to find Mr. Jenkins would be complicated and confusing. I arrived at his front door at exactly six o'clock.

The front door was attached to an aging old farmhouse that had been somewhat neglected. The boards on the outside walls needed a coat of paint; the porch furniture was well worn but still functional; and the flowerbed needed weeding.

Because the house belonged to an older gentleman, somewhere around seventy years old I was guessing his age to be, I understood the neglected condition of the outside of the house.

When Mr. Jenkins led me inside the house, I could see the same cared for but well-worn quality displayed everywhere in the crowded confines of the small living room.

"Mr. Jenkins, I'm Ellen Hutchins. Jim Thompson was my uncle."

"Yes ma'am. I talked to you on the telephone earlier today."

"I'm sure you know that Uncle Jim was murdered. I'm trying to talk to his friends and coworkers to see if I can find out why it happened?"

"That may not be a good idea," said Sam as he shook his head slowly from side to side to emphasize his negation.

"Why is that?"

"Jim Thompson was not liked by some people. He told me so himself," he said in a near whisper.

"Did he tell you why people didn't like him?'

"No," he answered hesitantly.

"He didn't tell you anything about who it was or why?"

"He said it was about the family of some big shot in Lebanon, one that had a lot of money, and he wanted his share."

"Do you know what family?"

"No, he certainly didn't tell me that. I thought, at first, he might have been involved in something illegal, but after I thought about it for a while, I changed my mind."

"Why?"

"I've known Jim Thompson for a long, long time. I'm seventy years old and Jim and I went to school together. He was a couple of years younger than me but we sat in the same room every day that we went to grade school," said Sam Jenkins as he paused to take a breath and wipe his watery eyes with a white handkerchief that he pulled from his hip pocket.

"Jim was hard to get to know, but I knew him. We worked together at the college as custodians for twenty years, until we both retired. He was my friend and he wouldn't have done anything illegal if he knew it was illegal. Jim didn't like to make trouble for himself or anyone else. He just wanted to be left alone to live his life the way he saw fit."

"Mr. Jenkins, I've never heard of Uncle Jim knowingly doing anything illegal either," I said to the old man as I tried to reassure him that I wasn't trying to tarnish Uncle Jim's memory.

"He was a good man," he said as he wiped at his watery eyes again.

"You've known him longer and better than anyone else I've talked with. Why did Uncle Jim have those young teenage boys living with him?"

"I can't answer that, young lady."

"You can't or you won't?" I probed.

"I can't. He never would tell me why he had them there."

"Do you think he was doing anything bad?"

"If you're asking me if he did nasty sex things with them, I'd say no. Jim wasn't that kind of man. He was a lonely man but not that lonely. He had them there for company. I'm sure of that."

"Can you think of anything else that I should know about Uncle Jim?'

"No, except that I miss him. He was my good friend," his voice broke with that statement so I decided to leave and let Mr. Jenkins keep his good memories.

My mind was having a hard time dealing with the statements Mr. Jenkins had made.

What family?

What big shot?

What money?

Uncle Jim was a bastard child as was my mother and Aunt Patti. My mother knew who her father was. I assumed it was the same man who fathered all three children. At least, I hoped that was the case. It was a much more pleasant thought that my grandmother loved and slept with one man whom she loved dearly even out of wedlock. I didn't want to believe that she spent her years lying down with many different men and bore three children with three different fathers.

Was that the case? Was my mom's dad the same man that fathered Uncle Jim?

My mother had told me that her father was a big shot in Lebanon whom she didn't care to know even though she knew who he was. Surely, Jim, if he had the same father, would also know the same information.

If they did have the same father who was the same big shot, what family was it? Why would it matter now?

My mother was dead.

Uncle Jim was dead.

Aunt Patti was the only other sibling living. Was she involved in this somehow? I always thought Aunt Patti should be the poster girl representing the redheaded stepchild. She didn't even remotely resemble Uncle Jim or my mother. If anyone possessed different parentage from my mom's father, it would be Aunt Patti.

I would have to visit Aunt Patti to see if she had anything to offer about Uncle Jim and why he had to die a violent death.

The ride home was eventful because I managed to get lost. Having been born with no sense of direction, it didn't surprise me that I would be floundering around in a rural world with which I was unfamiliar.

The county roads in Virginia could lead you to areas that should be avoided by most people, but especially by a single, white, female traveling alone in the darkness of the night.

The images of the hidden moonshine stills, even though they were fewer these days, played havoc through my mind. Moonshine and mountain folk seemed to travel hand in hand but the reality of today was that the moonshine stills as a moneymaker were replaced by marijuana plants representing the money crop.

Despite the fly overs by helicopters and small airplanes, the marijuana was continuing to grow, flourish, and be harvested for distribution. If, in your ignorance you stumbled over a marijuana field, your days would most likely be numbered in nothing beyond the present.

It was pitch black. There were no lights of any kind to be seen from businesses or houses. The moon, if there was one, was hidden from view by clouds. There was not even a pathetic street light anywhere within my line of vision.

Fear was creeping up my spine. I held my eyes wide open hoping to see something that looked the least bit familiar. Unless my headlights flashed on something, all that could be seen was black, forever black.

I had slowed my speed to a crawl. I needed a road sign, even a route sign or county road sign would do. I could then look it up on the map I had pulled out of the glove box to help me navigate to the tiny trailer that I wanted or needed to see so very much.

I thought I was backtracking on the same route that took me to see Mr. Sam Jenkins. I didn't know where I had made my mistake so I didn't know where I needed to make a correction.

I didn't know where I was.

I was scared.

A light, I saw a light. It was reflected in my rearview mirror so it must have been behind me.

It was gone. No more light could be seen.

"Wait a minute. There it is!" I shouted in the silent car.

It must be a vehicle traveling on the same road but some distance behind me. When I could see the light, the vehicle was cresting a hill. When the light disappeared, the vehicle had dived into a deep valley.

"What should I do? Should I wait for the vehicle to get to me? If so, I would pull over to the side of the road and just wait there," I asked myself as I stared at the rearview mirror. "Should I continue to drive to God knows where, until I reached lights and communities and people who could help me? What if this road just ended as many of them do in rural Virginia?"

I had not driven past one single house for what seemed like miles.

"Why would someone else be traveling this deserted, isolated road at night? I had a reason; I was lost. But why was I being followed? Who was it? Where did he come from? Where was he going?" I reasoned trying to avoid the all-consuming panic that was flooding through me.

I slammed on the brakes, threw the gear into park, and screamed. I needed a release. The pressure was building. My mind was ready to explode.

After gaining control of my scared self, I looked into my rearview mirror to see a vehicle racing up behind me with brightly flashing lights.

"A cop," I said in relief. "Thank God it's a sheriff's car that I was running away from."

I made no effort to move. I waited for the driver of the car that had pulled up and parked behind me to get off of his driver's seat and walk to the side of my car.

"You got a problem, lady?" asked a gruff sounding deputy.

"I sure do. I'm lost. I need to get back to Lebanon. How do I get there from here?"

"You need to turn around and drive in the other direction for a few miles. This road takes you to County Road 139. Take it for a couple more miles to Route 19. Then you have to turn right. Takes you right into town."

"What road am I on? Where does it go?"

"You're on Seiler Hollow Road. It takes you to the Big Bucket Coal Mine. Mine's been closed for a couple of years now."

"This road is in really good condition for the mine being closed, isn't it?"

"That's the way this county does things: repairs and maintains the unnecessary roads and leaves the well-traveled ones alone."

"Does anybody live around here?"

"Yeah, but they're pretty far off the road."

"I thought so. I never did see any lights on in a house. I would have stopped for directions."

"It's a good thing you didn't stop. Most folks around here don't take kindly to strangers, if you know what I mean."

"Yeah, I know. I don't sound local."

"Ellen Hutchins, isn't it? Your name I mean."

"Yes, but how did you know?"

"You're the talk of the town coming from the north and all."

"Who are you?"

"Deputy Stevenson, ma'am."

"You're the one who was supposed to meet me."

"That's what I've been told."

"Well, I can tell you now that it wasn't your voice I heard on the radio even if it was garbled."

"No, ma'am, it wasn't."

"Where can I turn around?"

"Just follow me. I'll show you."

"Oh, by the way, how come you're out on this God forsaken road to rescue me?"

"Got a call. It said someone was traveling real slow like they were looking for something or someone or they were lost. I was told to check it out."

"I'm glad you did, Deputy Stevenson. Thanks for your help."

"You're welcome. Just follow my car," he said as he walked back to his vehicle.

He pulled his car onto the road and drove past me to lead the way. He drove for a few moments then pulled over into a graveled area on the right where he made a sweeping curve and headed back into the direction from where we started.

I followed him until I came to County Road 139 where I had to turn to get back to Lebanon. I knew I was finally headed in the right direction so I wasn't so scared anymore.

At the first sign of lights blazing in the Town of Lebanon, I breathed an enormous sign of relief.

When I pulled into the driveway that led to the trailer, I was so happy I wanted to cry.

CHAPTER 17
DESTINED TO BECOME STRANGERS

Tuesday morning arrived like an unwelcome visitor. After spending a great deal of Monday evening trying to find my way home, I wasn't ready to go to work and be happy about it.

I had planned to call my Aunt Patti the night before, but when I got home from being lost, it was too late to disturb her. I would use my long distance calling card and call her from work.

I liked Aunt Patti and I thought Aunt Patti liked me despite the fact that I didn't particularly care for Aunt Patti's two daughters.

Things seemed to have changed after my mother died. That small feeling of family that had been present at the funeral completely disappeared. The tie that bound us, my mother, no longer existed. We were destined to become strangers.

It was hard for me to believe, but processing mortgage loan applications and the necessary paperwork had become boring and routine for me. The constant shuffling of the same forms, day after day, brought on moments of daydreaming.

All daydreams were not necessarily sprightly visions of loveliness and light. In my case, a daydream could easily transform itself into a nightmare.

My mind wandered upon the question of why Uncle Jim had an attachment to or an attraction for young men, teenagers.

I saw boy after boy enter Uncle Jim's house through floating scenes of a daydream. Each boy would glide to the front door and knock. It wasn't a normal knock and the boy didn't walk. He appeared to hover in the air barely above the ground. The knock on the door was more like an apprehensive tap.

Uncle Jim would pull the door open and bow deeply to the boy waiting at the door. Uncle Jim would then step to the side and motion for the young man to enter through the doorway. A sinister ugly smile would shine brightly on Uncle Jim's face as he closed the door before the next boy stepped forward to knock.

The boys were zombie like with their eyes staring at nothing and their movements slow and lethargic.

I saw them one after another enter the house when beckoned to do so by my evil Uncle Jim.

"Ellen, you have a call on line two," shouted a voice coming from the telephone intercom sitting on my desk.

I blinked myself back to reality while I cursed myself for jumping to conclusions.

"This is Ellen. May I help you?"

"You sure can," said a cheerful voice trying to talk above the background noise that surrounded him.

"It sure is good to hear your voice," I said as I could feel myself smile inside and out.

"Is there anything wrong?"

"No, nothing except that I miss you."

"I'll be back late tonight. Can I come by to see you?" he asked hesitantly.

"Sure you can. Please come by."

"It'll be really late, probably about one in the morning."

"I don't care what time it is when you get back. I want to see you, Tom," I said in a whisper because Mr. Crown was walking into my office.

"You have a visitor?" questioned Tom when he heard my whisper.

"Yes sir."

"I'll see you later, Ellen."

"That will be fine, sir," I whispered as quietly as I could.

I hung up the receiver and acknowledged the presence of Mr. Crown.

"I'm sorry for the interruption, Ellen, but I need to talk to you."

"All right," I answered as I felt a cold chill run down my spine.

"I'm going to close the door, if you don't mind."

"That's fine."

"Ellen, I've been receiving some telephone calls about you that have really started to concern me."

'Oh, God, what now?' I thought as I felt all of the color drain from my body.

"What kind of telephone calls?"

"A deputy sheriff has called me twice asking questions about you. Personal questions that I couldn't answer. Is there a problem, Ellen?"

"What were the personal questions?"

"Things like, who were your friends? Are you dating anyone? Things like that."

"Mr. Crown, you know I moved here from Ohio a few months ago. I have very few friends and I've gone out one time on a date. You can tell that to the deputy when he calls you again." I said as I felt the heat of anger rising to the top of my head.

"I don't intend to tell the deputy anything, Ellen."

"Which deputy was it? What was his name?"

"I don't remember what he told me his name was off hand. What's this all about?"

"Mr. Crown, all I can tell you is that my uncle was murdered in Richard County a few months ago while I was living in Ohio. I moved here because I inherited the Richard County land with the death of both my mother and my uncle. I wanted to live on that land and replant the roots that were pulled from the ground years ago when my mother left Virginia. I asked a few questions about my uncle's death and I have had nothing but trouble since the first question was asked."

"Well, I want you to know, Ellen, that it doesn't look good when a bank employee is being checked out by the legal authorities. I did have one other telephone call requesting information about you."

"Who was that one from?" I said with a bit of sarcasm.

"He said he was from the FBI."

"The FBI? There is no reason in the world for the FBI to be questioning me. Are you sure it was the FBI?"

"No, I talked to him on the phone. Anybody could tell me he was from the FBI and I wouldn't know the difference. There is no way to check a person's identification on the telephone."

"I don't know why they are doing this, Mr. Crown. I haven't done anything wrong except ask questions," I explained as I fought the tears that were flooding my eyes.

"This has to stop, Ellen. It could cost you your job."

"Why? I've done nothing wrong."

"It makes the bank look bad like I told you. You know we can't have that."

When I had nothing else to say in response, he stood and briskly walked out of my office closing the door behind him.

"God," I prayed softly, "I will never again ask you what's next."

It was lunchtime and I had had enough of the bank and its understanding and sensitive personnel. I laughed when I thought about those descriptive phrases.

As I walked out the door, I told the receptionist I was not feeling well and that I was leaving for the day.

I drove directly to the trailer where I called my Aunt Patti.

"Patti, this is Ellen Hutchins. How are you?"

Aunt Patti hesitated a moment before answering my question about her health.

"I'm fine. Why do you ask?"

Her tone told me that she wasn't happy that I had called.

"It's what normal people do when they start a conversation," I answered sarcastically. "It's my way of being polite."

"I'm sorry, Ellen. I didn't mean to snap at you. I'm a little out of sorts since everyone started dying. First your mom, then Jim. I thought maybe you were thinking I was next."

"As a matter of fact, Aunt Patti, I am thinking you might be next."

"What do you mean?" she asked anxiously.

"Are you going to be home this afternoon?"

"Yes."

"Is it all right for me to drive to Blacksburg to see you? It will take me a couple of hours to get there, but I don't want to talk about this over the telephone."

"Why not?"

"Strange things have been happening to me since I moved here to Richard County. I'm beginning to think my phone may be tapped. I know I'm being watched."

"I'll be home all afternoon, Ellen. You can come on but don't be bringing me any trouble I don't need."

"I'm leaving now. I should be there in two hours. If you haven't heard from me by seven o'clock this evening, you might want to call the state troopers and see if they can find me along the side of the road."

"What's going on, Ellen?"

"I don't know, Aunt Patti. I really need to talk to you. I really need to find out if you can help me get out of this mess."

"I'll watch for you, Ellen. If you have any kind of trouble getting here, call me and I'll come get you."

"Thanks, Aunt Patti. See you soon.'

I hung up the receiver, grabbed my handbag and keys, and was on my way to Blacksburg to talk to Aunt Patti.

It was midday. The sun was high in the sky giving up so much light that I had to squint from the brilliance.

I glanced up at my rearview mirror every few seconds to see if the same vehicle remained behind me for an extended length of time. In this rural area, it was likely that I could be followed by the same car for twenty or thirty miles. I was traveling the main thoroughfare that would take me from small town to small town. It was the route that everyone else traveling from town to town would follow.

"How was I going to know if I was being followed?" I whispered as I glanced up at the mirror.

Maybe when I got to the four-lane highway I would be able to check out the cars behind me a little more carefully.

I was driving in pick-up truck territory. It seemed that every other vehicle I passed or that passed me was a pick-up truck. The SUV was the next multiple vehicle model that was constantly present.

Farming and status were the reasons for the pick-up trucks. If the truck was not used in the family business, it was spit polished and protected from scratches and work wear for appearance sake. Many of the young men in the area treated their pick-up trucks like they were their best pair of dress shoes. They wanted no scuffs or signs of wear anywhere to be seen. On several occasions, I believe the trucks were being treated better than their wives and children. Heaven help the child that dropped a sticky sucker onto the upholstery.

I liked to drive cars- small cars. Pick-up trucks and SUV's were like driving armored tanks in my opinion.

I had always been a firm believer that driving a vehicle, any kind of four-wheeled chariot, was tantamount to carrying a gun. I considered a vehicle as dangerous, if not more dangerous, than a gun. A vehicle could kill as many people as a loaded gun with an equal amount of effort.

Of course, with the lethal weapon attitude in mind, you could bet that I was a cautious, speed-limit-follower type of driver.

I drove out of town onto the four-lane and was relieved that I wasn't being followed.

It would be a good day for a leisurely drive.

CHAPTER 18
I DON'T KNOW ANYTHING ABOUT DUBLIN

I pressed the dashboard button that would bring the radio to life. I wanted to hear something I could sing along with and enjoy as I tried to take my mind off the cloud of confusion that was constantly hovering over my head like a thorny crown.

I glanced in my rearview mirror and saw a car behind me. It wasn't the same car I had seen a few seconds before so I felt safe.

My mind was mulling over what I wanted to say to Aunt Patti. I didn't want to frighten her any more than I already had, but I did want Aunt Patti to be aware that there might be danger ahead.

I glanced at the rearview mirror again and there was a different car behind me. Beyond the car that was directly behind my car was a red SUV. I knew I had seen that SUV a couple of times when I glanced at the mirror.

My body tensed with the realization that I was being followed again. I held onto the steering wheel, grasping it so tightly that my knuckles were turning white.

I glanced at the large green signs with white letters above my head across the roadway listing the streets for the next exit.

"Maybe I should get off the freeway," I thought as I slowed my speed a bit so I could read the signs a little better.

Nothing looked familiar.

"Dublin, I don't know anything about Dublin. Was it a big town or little wide spot in the road? If I took that exit would I be able to lose my follower? Or, would I be running myself into a trap with no possible exit?" I asked myself more answerless questions.

I swerved my car suddenly to get onto the exit. My last minute decision prevented my follower from coming after me without causing a major pile up. I raced down the exit ramp to the end where I searched for the signs that would lead me back to the same freeway.

I slowly drove up the entrance ramp searching the cars in front of me for the red SUV that I had seen. I saw the vehicle exit on the next ramp. I knew the driver would get off the freeway so he could turn around and head back to the exit I had used to leave the freeway.

I continued driving to Aunt Patti's house without a sign of any more followers.

I wanted to laugh and shout and brag about my little stunt, but I had no one to share the news with, at least, not yet.

I wanted my followers, my enemies, my unknown foes, to reveal themselves so that I could see who or what I was fighting.

I wanted a reason that I could try to understand.

I wanted an explanation for why me? Had I asked the wrong question? Had I talked to the wrong person? Had I made a mistake moving to Richard County?

The joyful, bragging feeling I had been wanting to share was fading rapidly. Depression and despair were trying to overtake my life. I worked on channeling my mind to a better topic for thought.

None could be better than Tom, my Tom Walker. That sounded so good in my mind that I had to hear myself say it out loud.

"My Tom Walker. I can't wait to see you."

I was talking to myself again and I was liking what I was saying.

"What would people think if they saw me or heard me rattle on to no one else in the car with me? Oh, well, who cares what they think? It only matters about what I think, and about what Tom thinks," I said happily.

Aunt Patti was waiting for me. I no sooner had pulled into Aunt Patti's driveway until Aunt Patti had her front door open and was hurrying to meet me.

"Hi, Aunt Patti. How are you doing?" Ellen said without thinking about the previous time that she had asked the same question.

"Come in, Ellen. I'll get you something to eat and drink."

I glanced around to see if there was anyone or anything close enough to me and my car to be accused of following me.

Aunt Patti had prepared a meal fit for royalty for the two of us. I ate like I hadn't seen food for days while Aunt Patti picked at the small amount of food she had on her plate.

"What's going on in Richard County, Ellen?"

"That's what I would like to know. There have been some really weird things going on there."

"Like what?"

"Well, right after I arrived in the county, a man chased me out of the barn where Uncle Jim was killed. I was in the barn because that was the place I stored most of my belongings that I didn't need right away. He chased me up the mountain and I had to hide up there for several hours until it was almost dark.

"Then, when I asked the sheriff for help checking out the barn the next day, I didn't get the help that was supposed to be there. The deputy who was assigned to escort me to the barn didn't show up at the school where I was waiting for him.

"After that, I went out there again to check on my belongings and someone chased me again. I was sure he was trying to kill me. If he had gotten his hands on me it would have been all over. I had to run up the hill to try to get help from Maggie but she wasn't home. Fortunately, the guy chasing me didn't know she wasn't home. He was driving a red SUV. Do you know anybody who lives in Richard County that drives a red SUV?"

Patti shook her head from side to side indicating no.

"The sheriff has knocked on my door telling me that I shouldn't hire an out of town lawyer. I know my house is being watched or the sheriff wouldn't have known about the lawyer. I didn't hire that lawyer. He was and is a friend of mine.

"The preacher is condemning me for having an overnight visitor. I guess I'm going to hell for that. My friend has been staying with me because of all of the danger. I guess I'll just have to accept hell as my final destination because I'm not going to ask him to leave.

"I've been followed around town and on the way here. I managed to lose him today, so don't worry, Aunt Patti. You should have seen me leading that character down the road and then losing him when I swerved to an exit ramp at the very last second."

"Do you have any idea why?" asked an obviously concerned Aunt Patti.

"No, I don't have a clue. Do you know of any reason?"

"Why would I?"

"Just asking, Aunt Patti. I need help and I thought maybe you might have an idea."

The questioning was making Aunt Patti uncomfortable.

"Was she squirming because she knew something that she didn't want to talk about with me? Maybe she didn't know anything and was just afraid. I'd rather believe she was afraid," I told myself in my confused mind.

"Aunt Patti, I asked mom several times who her father was and she never would tell me. Do you know who it was?"

"What has that got to do with anything?"

"I don't know that it has anything to do with what is happening to me, but a friend of Uncle Jim's mentioned that Uncle Jim wanted his share of some money from the family of a Lebanon big shot. Do you know anything about that?"

"It can't be that, Ellen. The man is dead and has been for several years. So what if his family found out about his indiscretions with my mother, your grandmother? It was over long ago."

"Do you know who it was?"

"Yes."

"Are you going to tell me?"

"No, I don't think so."

Anger was rising in me but I knew I had to maintain control while talking with this elderly woman who was my aunt, my mother's sister.

"Why not?"

"You don't need to know, that's why not."

"How can you say that after you've heard about everything that has been happening to me? Mom told me that grandma was never married. Is that true?"

"That's what I was told," answered Patti impatiently.

"Who told you?"

"My mother, your grandmother."

"Did she tell you why she continued on with making illegitimate babies?"

"She loved him. That's all I know and all I care to know."

"That's not enough, Aunt Patti. I need to know the real truth."

"It's best to let sleeping dogs lie. In this case, it's best to let the past remain undisturbed."

"Okay, if you won't tell me who it was that fathered my mother, can you tell me if you all had the same father?"

"No, I can't. I'm assuming we did."

"You don't look like mom or Uncle Jim. Why don't you look like them, Aunt Patti?"

"There are members of our family that I have taken after. The red hair goes back a generation or two. You've studied some genetics in school, Ellen. You know that can happen."

"I had to ask, Aunt Patti."

"I know. I asked my mother the same question when I was younger. I got the same kind of answer I gave to you."

Patti got us both a cup of coffee and I continued to poke and probe at her past.

"Do you know why Uncle Jim never married?"

"He looked after mom."

"That's no reason to not get married, is it?"

"Mom was very demanding. She didn't want Jim out of her sight or off the property for any reason unless she was with him."

"Why was she like that with him? It didn't stop you and my mom from leaving home."

"Jim was the man of the house and she didn't want him to leave. She needed him to look after her in her old age. She needed him to look after the house and tend to the animals."

"Didn't he ever want to leave?"

"No, I don't think so. I don't think she allowed him to think that he could leave. Then as she got older, he wouldn't leave her alone."

"Was Uncle Jim gay?"

"No, never. Why would you think that?"

"He never married. As far as I know, he never even dated. He always had young boys hanging around the place. Why did he have those boys there?"

"He was lonely, Ellen. He enjoyed the company of males. He never had many friends, especially when his," our, mother was alive. I don't think he wanted to share his life with another woman after mom died. He was afraid all women were like our mother."

"Where did those boys come from?"

"They were boys who had run away from families in the area. Maybe they weren't from Richard County exactly, but they were from surrounding counties. If a boy showed up at Jim's house, he would make that boy contact his parents and tell them where he was and why."

"He was only trying to help them. Is that what you're saying?"

"Yes, but he also wanted their company for at least a little while."

"I'm glad to hear you say that, Aunt Patti. I didn't want to believe he was gay but there were some signs pointing me in that direction."

"Where did you get all those crazy notions?'

"Talk around the area. The sheriff, the preacher, all those I have talked to hinted at it."

"Don't believe it, Ellen. It isn't true."

"What about the house being burned down? Do you know anything about that?"

"Just what the sheriff told me and what I read in the Lebanon News."

"When was it in the paper?"

"The next week after it happened. The paper is published only once a week."

"You don't know why anyone would burn down the old school house and the home place. Is that right?"

"No, I can't think of a thing."

"What did Uncle Jim keep stored in the school house?"

"Junk. Whatever couldn't fit into the house, he put in the school house."

"Did you ever go in there?"

"Yes, it was junk just like I said."

"He never would let any of us in there. I was always curious about it."

"It was a bunch of old papers. That's all it was. Nothing important."

"Did you ever look at the old papers?"

"No, I never had any reason to do that. Besides, Jim was very possessive and obsessive when it came to his things. He didn't want anyone to touch them."

"Where did he keep his important papers?"

"I don't know. I guess he kept them in the house. Maybe in the old school house. Why do you ask?"

"He was supposed to have proof about who his father was. Where would he have kept the proof?"

"I don't have any idea."

"I wish you would tell me who my grandfather was or is. I think his identity has a lot to do with this whole mess. In my mind, the more people you tell, the safer you would be. Whoever is out to hurt me can't hurt everybody that knows the truth. The more people that know the truth, the better off we both are."

"The man is dead, Ellen. Why would it matter?"

"I don't know but I'm going to find out one way or another, Aunt Patti. I can promise you that."

I drank my coffee and talked with Aunt Patti about her two daughters and their families. Around eight o'clock, I decided I had better start driving back to Richard County. I wanted to make sure I was home when Tom arrived. I really wanted to see him, to talk to him, and to love him.

CHAPTER 19
TAP-TAP-TAP

I was glad to say that the drive back to the trailer from Blacksburg was uneventful. Constantly looking over my shoulder to see what kind of trouble was behind me was getting on my nerves.

I arrived at the trailer a couple of minutes after midnight. I showered and dressed in a lounging outfit I had never worn previously and waited for Tom to arrive.

I turned on the television to help me pass time and to cover the night sounds that I couldn't identify.

I saw headlights flash momentarily in my living room window. It must have been a passing car because the lights disappeared. I heard no car engine turn off and no Tom came knocking at my door.

I saw headlights again but no other sounds to indicate that I had a visitor.

There was no reason for that kind of traffic activity on this road at this late hour. I was most likely being watched again. The sheriff's department was out on patrol, doing their thing, trying to scare me into running away, leaving the town.

"But why? Why would they want to antagonize me so much? What is it that they wanted from me?" I asked my tired, overworked mind. "Maybe it wasn't the sheriff this time. But who could it be and why?"

I, once again, talked myself into being scared.

I rose from my sofa and turned off the television so I could hear every sound being made around me. I didn't want to hide the night sounds any longer. I wanted to identify each and every one of them.

I needed something with which to protect myself. I went to the drawer in the kitchen where I had hidden most of my tools. I grabbed a hammer. Holding it firmly in my right hand, I wanted to be ready to swing it in a fraction of a second.

I walked to the far end of the small trailer where I stood in the middle of the bedroom with the lights extinguished. I listened intently for any unfamiliar noise such as footsteps, a barking dog, the shuffling of leaves, anything that I thought I should know about so I could put up a proper defense.

I heard a tapping sound. It was so light a tap that I almost couldn't hear it.

I closed the bedroom door to block light from any other part of the trailer and I listened again.

Tap-tap-tap was coming from the side of the trailer next to the window. I walked to the window and opened the blinds so I could see what was outside.

I heard it again. The tap-tap-tap was intermittent but it hadn't stopped. I moved a slat on the mini blind so I could peer outside at the total blackness.

"There must not be a moon," I thought as I saw nothing but blackness.

Tap-tap-tap and then the sound of a moan.

I clutched the hammer tighter as I put my left hand together with my right hand on the handle. I was ready, willing, and able to let anybody have it with that weapon.

The tap-tap-tap got louder and the moan became a long sound almost like a low-pitched whistle.

I felt my knees start to give way as I realized what I was hearing.

"It's the wind!" I shouted as I relaxed my grip on the hammer.

I heard a noise, a car maybe, as I raced from the bedroom to the living room.

The doorknob was being twisted and a body was gently shoving against the door.

"Ellen, are you in there?" said a voice barely above a whisper.

"Tom?"

"Yes, it's Tom. Open the door."

I opened the door while I was still holding the hammer.

"Is there anything wrong, Ellen?"

"Not anymore," I said as I threw the hammer onto the sofa and wrapped my arms around him.

"I love the greeting, Honey, but please tell me what's wrong."

I looked at him and I couldn't stop myself from kissing him longingly and lovingly. I knew as soon as we pulled away from each other that I was going to burst into tears.

"I'm so glad you're back," I said between sobs.

"Honey, what's wrong?" he asked me with evident concern.

"Everything and nothing, Tom," I said as I tried to stop the sobbing.

"Take a deep breath and tell me what's been happening," he said as he led me to the sofa. He moved the hammer that had landed on the seat cushion and we sat side by side as he tried to console me.

"I'm scared, Tom. I've been followed, chased, and watched. I don't know why this is happening," I said as the gush of tears began anew.

"I'm here, Honey. I'm not going to leave. I promise you," he said as he held me close to him.

"I can't ask you to stay with me. What if something happened to you? God, Tom, it would be my fault. No, you can't stay."

"I am and I already have some of my clothes in the car. I had to be out of town yesterday and today but I'm here to stay until this is over and we find out what's going on," he said firmly.

"I love you, Tom."

"I know. You've loved me for a long time, with each little phone conversation, with each little insult, with each little dig you made at me and to me on the telephone soon after you started working at the bank. I've loved you back just as much."

Finally, the tears stopped.

Tom retrieved his suitcases from the car, carried them into the bedroom, and we went to bed huddled up against one another.

No sex was needed. We each wanted only to know that the other one was there.

Seven o'clock dropped onto them quickly and the alarm let them know loudly that the night was done.

Even though we had no need to be physical when we went to bed, when the alarm sounded the next morning, we attacked each other like love-starved animals. We weren't love starved for long at that point in time.

When we were expended, we resumed our conversation of the previous night.

"I went to see a man named Sam Jenkins. He lives in Belfast and he was my uncle's best friend. Maybe he was Uncle Jim's only friend."

"Did you find out anything from him? By the way, before you answer that, you shouldn't be doing all the question asking alone, you know."

"I know, but I just can't sit on my hands. I've got to do something. Anyway, Mr. Jenkins said Uncle Jim knew something, a secret, and he wouldn't tell anybody what the secret was. At least, that was what I understood him to mean."

"Did Mr. Jenkins threaten or scare you in any way?"

"No, no, he was a nice old man who was real sad about losing his best friend. The scary part happened after

I left Mr. Jenkins," I said as I paused to get my thoughts in order.

"Okay, give. What happened?"

"I got lost after I left Mr. Jenkins. I was on this road that led to a mine that was closed and when I started to get panicky and really frightened, a deputy sheriff appeared out of nowhere."

"Why would that scare you?"

"We were the only two cars on that road for miles and miles. If he wasn't following me, then someone else was and that someone else called the deputy. Actually, that was what he said. He said someone reported my slow moving car was possibly lost. Seems awful convenient to me."

"Yeah, it would be hard to believe that it wasn't staged."

"That's what I thought."

"Okay, what else?"

"At work, Mr. Crown threatened me with unemployment if people who identified themselves as deputies continued to question Mr. Crown about me."

"Is that it?"

"No, I called my Aunt Patti who lives in Blacksburg and then I drove to her house yesterday. I left work early so I could talk to her and get back here before you arrived."

"Did anything happen?"

"I was followed by a red SUV. I managed to lose him by making a last second decision to get off the interstate. I jumped right back on at the entrance next to the same exit I used, and watched the red SUV leave the interstate on the very next exit while I remained on the interstate and drove on to Aunt Patti's without an escort."

"I'm proud of you for losing that tail but you should have waited for me. I would have gone with you."

"I know. I'm sorry."

"Why were you holding a hammer when I got here?"

"I heard a noise and managed to scare myself silly. That's all that was. I promise."

"You've had a really rough couple of days."

"I don't care to repeat them. I can tell you that much."

"I'm going to the courthouse today."

"In Stillwell County?"

"No, here in Richard County. I want to do some research on your property."

"Don't you have to work today?"

"No, they think I'm still in Richmond. I'm not going to tell them anything different."

"What can I do to help you?"

"Nothing, except to write down on a piece of paper your great-grandmother's name, your grandmother's name, your mother's name, and your name. I want to see what I can find on any of them. I also need your Aunt Patti's and Uncle Jim's full names."

"Is that all you need?"

"For now, to get me started. You go ahead and get ready for work. Have you got an extra key to the front door?"

"No, but I'll get one made today. I do have one for the back door. You can have it until I get you a key to the front door."

I rushed around getting myself dressed and ready to face Mr. Crown.

Tom dressed in blue jeans and a sport shirt. We parted company with a lingering kiss at the front door.

I drove towards Richlands and Tom drove towards downtown Lebanon.

CHAPTER 20
YOU HAVE SOME POWERFUL ENEMIES

When I arrived at the bank, Mr. Crown was waiting for me.

"Ellen, I need to speak to you."

"Yes sir," I said as I sighed with frustration.

I entered his office and he motioned for me to close the door.

"Ellen, I'm sorry I have to tell you this, but your services are no longer needed at this bank."

I stared at him without blinking my eyes while my jaw hung open to display my shock. It took a few moments for me to fully process what he had said to me.

"Why?" I uttered in total disbelief.

"You have some very powerful enemies, Ellen."

"Why are you firing me? Give me a reason," I pleaded.

"The board has directed me to do this. I don't have any choice."

"Did they give you a reason?"

"The FBI, the sheriff's office, and I don't know who else have managed to get the bank board members up in arms. You need to clear out your desk. Leave everything you haven't finished where I can find it. We will mail your final check to you."

I stood up and walked out of the room. I walked to my office, gathered my personal belongings into a plastic bag, and walked out of the bank never to return.

I got into my car, started the engine, and drove long enough to get away from the parking lot and the sight of this horrendous mental anguish I was suffering.

"Now what, God? What do I do now?" I cried as I
sat in the Hardees parking lot.

I pulled a tissue from my handbag, checked myself
in the rearview mirror, then I took off for Richard County
where I would hopefully find some answers.

I drove directly to the trailer where I changed into
blue jeans and a tee shirt.

I visited the hardware store in Lebanon where I had
a key to my front door made for Tom to use.

I went to the courthouse in search of Tom to see if I
could help him help me.

The courthouse was an old structure dating back to
the turn of the twentieth century. There were small
cubicles and large offices throughout the structure allowing
for many nooks and crannies in which a body could be
standing or sitting.

I started my search in the deed room that also
housed the copies of the last will and testaments of the
deceased Richard County residents.

When my search yielded no sign of Tom, I spotted a
clerk who wasn't busy with another customer or client and
questioned her.

"I'm looking for Tom Walker. He is an attorney
from Stillwell County who is researching some real estate
matters here. Have you seen him?"

"What does he look like? I don't remember the
name."

"He's about six feet tall with sandy brown hair and
glasses. He's got a very distinctive voice. It's very deep
and melodious."

"No, I don't think he's been in here today."

"He was wearing blue jeans. He has only one good
arm," I added for emphasis.

"Then he's definitely not been in here," said the
clerk who appeared to be getting impatient with me.

"You're sure?"

"Yes ma'am. I'm very sure. There's been no one in here that matches that description."

"Thank you," I said as I turned and walked away.

I couldn't imagine what could have happened to Tom. He told me he was going to the courthouse.

Maybe he called his office and then had to go take care of some business.

I had given him directions on how to get to the property. Maybe he drove to Dry Branch to check it out.

Maybe, maybe, maybe, I didn't want to guess anymore. I wanted to know where he was. I wanted to know that he was all right.

I ran to my car and started driving away from Lebanon going towards Dry Branch. I was driving at or below the speed limit looking everywhere as rapidly as I could. I searched small ravines and creek banks and mountain ledges trying to spot Tom's car. I was afraid someone might have run him off the road and left him for dead.

"God," I prayed, "don't let him be hurt."

When I reached the gate to the property I put the gear in "Park" and exited the car to open the gate. I drove the car through to the other side of the gate and parked so I could close the gate.

When I climbed back into my car, I caught a glint off of something shiny lying on the ground. I drove my car up as close as I could to the glinting object without running the tires over it. I leaned out of my car and picked it up. It was the key to the back door of my trailer.

"Tom is here or has been here," I said softly.

I straightened myself up behind my steering wheel and decided to drive down the hill.

I tried to avoid the areas that I knew would scrape the bottom of my low profile car, but I couldn't avoid all of them. While I was trying to dodge the bottom scrapers, I was also trying to find Tom.

I didn't see his car anywhere.

"How did he get here if he didn't drive? What happened to his car? What happened to him? Where is he?" I worried.

I winced each time my car scraped the uneven rutted road. I continued driving and I continued searching.

I turned right at the bottom of the first hill onto the wagon path that ran past the old burned out home place. I continued driving down that hill towards the barn.

As I drove past the tall weedy area that was once a garden, I saw his car. It was parked in front of the barn but the tall weeds had obscured my view of the vehicle.

I drove my car up next to Tom's car where I parked and climbed out of the driver's seat.

"Tom? Are you inside?" I shouted towards the barn.

The lock was still in place so there was no way for him to be inside the barn.

I walked to the side of the barn and looked towards the back of the building. I didn't see him. I walked completely around the barn and saw no signs that he had even been there, only that his car was parked in front of the barn.

"Tom? Where are you?" I shouted.

"Ellen, Ellen, I'm down here."

It was Tom, but where was the voice coming from.

"Ellen, come down to the corn crib. I need your help."

I started running. The corncrib was down the hill a few hundred feet further than the barn and it was off to the left.

"Tom, where are you?" I asked as I stared at the corncrib. The structure was built with two sides that were connected only by the roof between them. The roof covered an open area in which Uncle Jim always parked his tractor to keep it out of the weather. The doors to each side of the corncrib were directly in the front of each side.

"Over on the left side. Come on in and give me a hand."

I yanked the door open and peered inside at the darkness while my eyes adjusted from the bright sunlight to the slatted dark interior of the corncrib.

"Over here, Ellen."

I walked inside to see Tom lying on the floor of the corncrib.

I ran to his side.

"Are you okay?"

"Yeah, someone knocked me on my hard head. I just have a bump about the size of Mount Everest, that's all," he explained as he rubbed the back of his head.

"Did you see who did it?"

"No, I didn't know anyone was in here until the lights went out after he hit me a good one."

"Let me help you up. We need to get you to the emergency room."

"No, I don't think so, Ellen. They won't do anything more for me than what you could do. I'd rather stay with you."

I helped him get to his feet but he wasn't ready to leave yet.

"Look over here, Ellen. I found an old wooden trunk. It's got a bunch of old papers in it. Let's take it to my car and we'll take it back to your place so we can see what these papers are."

"Okay, can you grab the metal handle on that end?" I asked as he reached up to touch the bump on his head.

"Sure, just give me a minute."

I walked up in front of Tom and put my arms around him.

"Lean on me, Tom."

"I'll be fine in a minute, Ellen. We need to get this trunk out of here."

I moved to the opposite end of the wooden trunk. He grabbed his end and we heaved the heavy object off of the rough floor of the corncrib.

He led the way as he backed out of the door. I slowly followed his lead until we were standing at the rear of his car.

He lowered his end of the heavy trunk to the ground so he could pull the keys from his pocket to open the car trunk. We lifted the battered old wooden trunk and placed it in Tom's car.

Before he put his keys back into his pocket, he started searching his pockets for something.

"Is this what you're looking for?" I asked as I held up the key I had found at the top of the hill.

"It sure is. Where did you find it?"

"At the top of the hill. When you came through and closed the gate, you must have dropped it. Did you get out of your car to look down the hill before you drove down to the barn?"

"No, I didn't. After I closed the gate, I didn't get out again until I got to the barn."

"That's funny. I didn't find it where you would park your car to close the gate. I found it further up the road, past the place where the old school house used to be."

"Maybe whoever hit me dropped it after he took it from me?"

"How long do you think you were unconscious? "

"Not long. Maybe a few minutes. What time is it?"

"It's about two in the afternoon."

"You're kidding."

"No, Tom. What time did you think it was?"

"About eleven in the morning."

"You must have been out a lot longer than you thought."

146

"Yeah, I guess so. What are you doing here? You're supposed to be at work," he asked as he tried to sort through the confusion that was clouding his brain.

"I was fired."

"You what?"

"Mr. Crown said the bank board directed him to let me go."

"Did he give you a reason?"

"Just that I had some powerful enemies. The board didn't like it because I was being investigated by the FBI and sheriff's office."

"That FBI thing can't be true, Ellen."

"That's what I thought but that is the second time it has been mentioned."

"Let's go home, Ellen. I'll have to check out the papers at the courthouse another day. I'll also make a couple of calls and see if the FBI is investigating you and, if so, why?"

"I'll follow you, Tom. Drive slow, okay?"

He climbed into his car and I climbed into my car.

We formed our own little convoy back to the trailer.

My mind wandered back to the key.

Why was it at the top of the hill? Tom had been knocked out long enough for someone to take it from him and go have a copy made. Rather than take a chance on Tom gaining consciousness while the original key was being returned, the thief probably threw it on the ground at the top of the hill trying to make it look like Tom had recklessly dropped it. That nut, that crazy person, that possible killer, could be walking around with a key to my home in his pocket.

CHAPTER 21
GATHERING ENEMIES

When we reached my small trailer, we parked both cars directly in front so they could be easily seen from the road. It was a bit of defiance on my part. Tom said it was because of a strong case of pride for him.

My first task upon entering the tiny trailer was to look around to see if anything had been disturbed. Nothing looked out of place. Maybe I was paranoid, but I wasn't going to take any chances.

"Tom, I'm going to wedge this chair back under the doorknob of the rear door just in case that nut made a copy of the key. I'm sure you didn't lose the key, not where I found it anyway."

"Good idea, Ellen. Let me help you."

I could see that Tom was beginning to see and feel the dangers that had been lurking around me. With his association with me, he had been pulled into something he didn't understand either.

I hoped that this sudden realization of danger wasn't going to scare him away because he was my only ally. I seemed to be gathering enemies everywhere I went in southwest Virginia. I prayed that Tom wouldn't become one of them.

I watched Tom closely all afternoon and evening. If he was going to suffer any affects due to the hit on the head, I wanted to know about them so I could drive him to the emergency room immediately. But, like he told me when I kept asking him how he was feeling, "I have a hard head, Ellen. I'll be okay."

I made something for us to eat and then we got down to looking at the contents of the wooden trunk.

When Tom raised the lid, smells of old paper, mildew, and dampness escaped from the musty interior filling up the small living room.

The papers were yellowed with age and some of them were disintegrating from our touch.

There were old photographs that were sepia colored. Some of the pictures had curled up while others looked as good as new.

I picked up a handful of the papers on the top of the pile and started looking through them.

"Ellen, do you know who these people are?" asked Tom as he held up a photograph for me to see.

"That one there was my grandma. The lady next to her was my great-grandma. See that long black dress she's wearing?" I asked as I pointed at the picture.

Tom nodded his head in answer to my question.

"She always wore a long black dress. The woman seemed to be in a perpetual state of mourning. I guessed she was mourning for the passing of my great-grandfather. I never knew him. He was dead and gone long before I was born."

"How old was she in that picture?"

"I don't have any idea. She was ninety-two when she died. She lived a long life."

"What did she die of?"

"When she was ninety-one, she was still traipsing around on the mountain. She stepped into a gopher hole, or the hole that led to the home of some kind of underground animal, that caused her to fall and break her hip. She never did get over that broken hip. She died a few months later."

"I don't suppose there was anything suspicious about her death?"

"Not that I know of. Old age is basically what killed her. Her parts were worn out and they stopped functioning."

"What about your grandmother? How old was she when she died?"

"Seventy-two was what my mom told me. I didn't go to the funeral. I don't remember why I didn't except that Grandma Thompson was not one of my favorite people."

"Why didn't you like her?"

"She played favorites with my two cousins, Sandy and Suzy. As a kid whenever we visited grandma, all she did was talk about those two cousins of mine. I guess I was a bit jealous. I know I got really tired of hearing about what Sandy didn't like and what Suzy did like. Of course, of those two girls, Suzy was favored because she was more of a tomboy and fun loving. Sandy was moody and hard to get along with. At least, that's what I heard my grandma tell mom.

"I remember one time I went running around to the back of the house and I saw my great-grandma with her long black dress pulled up so she could pee next to the house. She had backed her butt up to the side of the house, bent her knees slightly, and let it flow. The outhouse was just a few feet up a path near the back door, but she peed in the backyard. I remember that long, black dress and her white hair fastened with hairpins in the back to form a bun against the nape of her neck. I remember her gold wire-rimmed glasses sitting about half way down her nose. I remember nothing else about her except that for some reason known and understood only in the minds of children, I was afraid of her."

"She looks like she might have been a little on the stern side."

"I think she was. I don't think she wanted to be bothered by her great-grandchildren. She was getting too old to derive any pleasure from seeing us running around and interrupting her daily routine."

Rather than ask me about each picture one at a time, he chose to pile the pictures up separating them from the papers. He wanted to know who was in the photos, but he also wanted to read the contents of the papers.

We looked at old bills of sale for a few head of cattle, some sheep, some piglets and an old sow, plus a mule. I remembered my mother telling me they plowed the cornfield using an old mule that was stubborn and didn't want to pull the plow.

There were personal, handwritten letters from my mother to grandmother, from my mother to Uncle Jim, from Aunt Patti to grandma, and from Aunt Patti to Uncle Jim.

I set all of the letters of a personal nature aside. I would read them later to try to understand why my family was always so cold and distant.

"Tom, I want to read these so I'll put them in a separate box. My family was never, ever close. My dad had been married before and was thirteen years older than my mom so he wasn't welcomed into the family with the blessings of my grandma. I'd like to read these letters to see if anything changed during the years. I would like to think they mellowed with age and accepted dad and us, my brother and me, through the years. I never felt acceptance, but it would be nice to know it happened."

"From what you've told me about your grandma and her having three illegitimate children, she certainly had no right to condemn your mother's choice for a husband."

"You would think that, wouldn't you?"

We found copies of old land deeds with receipts for recording costs. There were old IOU's that had been marked 'PAID IN FULL'.

Tom piled up the land deed copies and anything related to legal issues in one pile.

There was a bill of sale handwritten saying that someone, the name had faded so much I couldn't read it, had purchased a female Negro and a buck Negro for the sum of two hundred dollars.

I stared at that receipt in wonder.

"I didn't know my family owned slaves, Tom."

"If you're from the south, Ellen, at one time or another, everyone's family owned slaves."

"No one ever told me about this."

"This bill of sale is really old. I'm sure it was forgotten by those family members who knew about it when you were a child and those people are now dead."

"It seems strange to think about owning slaves. I had no idea my family had enough money to buy slaves."

"You didn't have to have a lot of money to buy a slave. It was a really cheap way to get help on the farm. Only a one-time pay out was involved. You didn't have to hire any white person and pay him a daily wage if you could buy a slave. So, no, you didn't have to be rich, only smart."

"How come you know so much about buying slaves?"

"My family owned several slaves at one time. Like I said, if you're from the south, it's probably in your background somewhere."

"How are you feeling, Tom? Is your head hurting? Is there something I can do?"

"Sure is. Let's go to bed. We've been plowing through these pieces of history all evening and now it's almost midnight. I have to work tomorrow and you need to job hunt."

I was so glad he suggested bed. I was exhausted.

"Just leave everything scattered around. We'll look at this stuff again tomorrow."

After we each completed the nighttime ablutions, we kissed each other goodnight and rapidly fell asleep.

CHAPTER 22
SINKHOLE RUMORS

Tom hurried as he prepared himself for work. He had a much longer drive ahead of him than he was used to taking to the office every morning.

"I'll grab a cup of coffee on the way, Ellen. I'll see you this evening, probably around six. Please stay out of trouble. Okay?"

I puffed out my lower lip and tried to pout.

"I'm not the one who got hit on the head, was I?"

"You've got a point," he said as he kissed me on the cheek and hurried out the door.

He was gone and I was alone again. I pulled on my blue jeans and drove to the convenience store where I purchased more newspapers.

The job search would begin again.

It didn't take me long to discover that there were no employment opportunities suitable for me listed in the classifieds. I couldn't drive a truck or be a car mechanic.

I looked around my living room at the piles of photographs and old papers and vowed that I would look at or read every piece of paper scattered about on the floor.

When I saw a copy of an old bill of sale for land, it reminded me that, as far as I knew, I was the only living family member who was interested in living on the Thompson land. Everyone else lived out of town or out of state and had no interest in what happened to the property.

I wondered if the land was the focal point for the problems that I had been having. The land was undeveloped and unused. The tobacco allotment my uncle had held onto for years and years went to someone else on his death. He didn't actually use the allotment personally because he was too old and wasn't able to do the fieldwork anymore. He leased the land and allotment that remained in his name to another local farmer who paid him a flat fee every year for the use of the allotment and the land.

The only other notable attachment to the land I knew about was the sinkhole located just below the barn close to where grandma used to keep the hogs penned.

When I was a child, I was never allowed near the hogs. My mother told me they would knock me down and trample me.

What she was doing was scaring me away from the sinkhole.

There was a hog pen that was fenced for the protection of the hogs. Also, the pen was to keep from having to chase the hogs all over the farm and running the fat off of them.

There was a second fenced area that blocked people from stepping into the sinkhole and falling down into an underground cavern that probably crisscrossed the land for miles. The only problem with this particular sinkhole was that no one knew how deep it was.

My mother told me there had been rumors of people dropping the whole bodies of cattle in the sinkhole to hide the existence of a sickness or disease that affected the cows or bulls. The mouth of the sinkhole on my property wasn't big enough to do that, but the farmer next over had one that could accommodate a dead cow.

The rumors claimed that when the cow was dropped, you never heard it hit bottom. The hole was that deep.

Development in the area was non-existent. If you weren't farming the land or grazing cattle on it, it would rapidly be lost to brush and cedar trees.

It would be a good place to build a housing development because the rolling foothills to the mountains were beautiful during all four seasons. You had to keep in mind that you didn't want to build over a possible sinkhole.

My gut told me that my greatest enemy was the one who hit Tom on the head.

"Was it the same person that chased me both times?" I pondered. "Who was the guy? Why was he on my land? What connection did he have to my Uncle Jim? Did one man commit both offenses or were two separate men involved?"

I picked up the photographs and looked at them trying to identify our particular branch on my family tree.

Great-grandma Ella was a small woman. Her daughter, Molly who was my grandmother, was a large, raw-boned woman. She stood about five feet eight and was husky built, almost like a man; but she wasn't a man, she was my grandmother.

Every picture taken of Great-grandma Ella and Grandma Molly together in the same photograph showed no happiness in either face. No photograph in the pile when they were together displayed a smile on either woman.

I had no idea what Great-grandma Ella's maiden name was, nor did I have any idea what my great-grandfather's name was. I could find no pictures labeled with a reference to him even though there were photographs of men in the pile on the floor.

I found pictures of my mother, Winnie, Aunt Patti, and Uncle Jim when they were young. There weren't many of those three, but enough to know that they were legitimate family members.

I found pictures of Sandy and Suzy. There were lots of photos of those two and very few of Lee and me. My mother and father weren't into picture taking very much.

I eliminated all of the recognizable family members by placing them in a separate stack leaving those I wasn't able to identify for further research. I shoved the photographs of people I didn't know into my handbag.

The telephone rang and startled me from my thoughts.

"Ellen, how are you doing?"

"I'm fine, Tom. There weren't any job listings for me in the newspapers so I started going through the stuff we have scattered on the floor."

"Then how's that coming along?"

"Fine, I'm just looking at the photographs right now. I thought I would separate the ones I could identify from the ones I had no clue about. I want to do some checking with Aunt Patti and the sheriff and maybe Preacher Johnson to see if they might know these people."

"Well, don't do any checking without me, okay?"

"Okay."

"I'm trying to get the next couple of days off so I can do some research at the courthouse. I've got to take care of a few things today and that should clear my calendar for Friday and Monday."

"That's great, Tom. It sure would be nice to find some answers."

"I'll see you later, Ellen. Don't go snooping without me. You promise?"

"I promise," I said as I fought the urge to be annoyed. It was nice to be cared about, but it was also frustrating. I had been doing things on my own for so long without having to consider the feelings of anyone else that it was hard for me to adjust to considering the feelings of someone else now.

I liked to be cared for and about but I didn't like having to report my every move or having to ask permission to make a move.

My mind wandered back to Uncle Jim's death.

"Did one of his boys kill him? Did he do something so bad that he had to be killed? Did he promise something to one of them and not keep his word? Why were they there? Who were they? Where did they go after he died? Did they go? Are they still there? Are they hiding and living off of the land? Who or what are they hiding from?" swirled the questions.

I had to shut my mind off. I had to stop the questions that were floating around unanswered before they drove me crazy.

I picked up some of the papers that were of no value and all of the photographs in which I could identify all of the people and threw them into a box. I carried that box into the bedroom where I stored it in the closet.

I had a lot of time before Tom would get back from Stillwell. I was going to drive to Lebanon to check out the newspapers. Maybe I could find something about both the murder and the fires.

The Lebanon Times was a small office for a small town newspaper. The printing of the newspaper wasn't actually done on the spot. It was jobbed out to a printer in Abingdon.

"I'm Ellen Hutchins," I explained to the lady sitting at the front desk when I entered the office. "I just recently moved to Dry Branch and I would like to see some of your old newspapers from about ten months ago."

"I'm sorry, ma'am, we don't have them here. You will need to go to the Lebanon Library."

"You don't archive any of your newspapers?"

"You mean do we have any of the old copies? Is that what you're asking?"

"Yes, it is."

"We have some laying around and boxed up but they aren't in any particular order. The library microfilms them and if we need to look up anything, that's where we go."

"Thanks, I guess I'll go to the library then."

The library was a one-story building that had spread out as additional rooms were added at odd angles.

The first thing I had to do was get a library card. It was funny how that library card made me feel more and more like I belonged to the neighborhood. I no longer felt the sense that I was on the outside of a locked gate trying to gain access. At least, I had my foot partially inside the door.

"I need to look at some of your old Lebanon Times newspapers from several months ago," I said to the middle-aged lady wearing a head of tightly curled gray hair behind the front desk.

"Marcy, show this lady where the microfilm of the newspapers are kept," responded the librarian without a hint of a smile.

"Thank you," I whispered to the librarian as I walked away following Marcy.

Marcy demonstrated the viewing machine for the microfilmed newspapers. She then left me to my own devices.

I went back a year and paged through each small newspaper until I reached the announcement of Uncle Jim's death. I printed a copy of the obituary for my records and then started backtracking to find the page or pages that mentioned his murder.

I didn't know how I had missed them. When I started at the beginning of the same newspaper in which his obituary was listed, I noticed that a page was missing. In the area where the page should have been displayed, an obvious splice in the microfilm could be seen.

"Marcy, do you know what happened to this page?" I asked when I caught her attention.

"Let me see," she said as she stood behind me peering over my shoulder at the machine. "Oh, yeah, I remember that. I found that one in the machine one day with the broken microfilm. I don't know who did it, but I repaired it the best I could."

"You don't have a copy of this newspaper anywhere else, do you?"

"No, but the newspaper office might have one. Write down the date and I'll call them for you."

"Thanks, I would really appreciate your doing that.'

I continued looking at the old newspapers until I got to the articles about the fires.

There wasn't much mentioned except that the house appeared to be an accidental fire while the schoolhouse fire was set by vandals. There was no mention of a fire marshal or any other investigating officer involved.

I copied those two small articles for my files.

I decided, just for my own curiosity, to travel back many years in the newspaper microfilms. I looked for names that were familiar to me and resemblances to any of the old photographs I had placed in my handbag.

I was randomly picking out years and writing the years chosen into a notebook. After I finished viewing this time, I would come back again and view some more. I was more interested in the newspaper photographs than anything else, but I didn't see any that were familiar in the years I had chosen.

On my way out of the library, I glanced at the old photographs hanging on the wall that were of the founding fathers of the Lebanon Library.

I made a mental note to look at any portrait pictures hanging in the public buildings such as the courthouse.

No mention was made of whether the newspaper office had a copy of the article I was looking for by either librarian.

I drove back to the tiny trailer with my mind reviewing everything that had been happening.

As soon as I arrived at the trailer, I located my tape recorder and added to my dictation of the events since my talk with my cousin, Maggie.

I wanted to make sure I chronicled the events as they happened so that if there were any questions in the future, I would have the information at my fingertips.

I finished dictating my life story and hid the tape in the breaker box.

I went into the kitchen to find something to prepare for us to eat. Spaghetti was about it for my stock of food supplies. I would have to remedy that problem over the weekend or we would be eating out for every meal.

CHAPTER 23
SEARCHING FOR THE TRUTH

Friday morning, we climbed out of bed with our minds set on a mission.

Tom was going to check out the chain of ownership for the property. He was also going to obtain copies of any of the wills that were on record.

He wanted me with him in case he had any questions, but he also wanted me to drive my own car so that he could go in one direction while I went another when we searched for the truth.

We were standing on the courthouse steps at eight o'clock waiting to get in and start the record search.

He started in the late eighteen hundreds which would have been around the time Great-grandma Ella was born.

My not knowing my great-grandma's maiden name made it difficult to go back that far so he focused on the years where he thought she would be a teenager and moved forward.

He was looking for a marriage license or some kind of registry that indicated who married whom.

None could be found.

I was sure my Great-grandma Ella had been married but no record was forthcoming. Then I thought about it some more and remembered there was no great-grandfather for me to remember. Supposedly, he was dead and gone long before I came into the picture.

He couldn't find a birth record.

He couldn't find a record of marriage.

The next step was the Last Will and Testament of Ella Thompson. He found the will and purchased a copy of it for us to keep.

"Ellen, according to Ella Thompson's Will, she skipped right over your Grandmother Molly leaving her only a life estate in the land."

"Yes, that's what I was told."

"Why would she do that?"

"I guess that she didn't want my grandmother to sell the land. If she tied it up the way she did, Grandma Molly was stuck."

"After your grandmother died, her children-meaning your mother, your Uncle Jim, and your Aunt Patti-could have sold the property."

"By the time Grandma Molly died, Uncle Jim was getting up in years and he had lived there all of his life. Aunt Patti, I've been told, signed her rights to the land over to Uncle Jim but my mom didn't. It didn't matter because Uncle Jim had no intention of selling the land. He just wanted it to be his and his only."

"How much property was involved?"

"I don't really know. Uncle Jim had bought a couple of small pieces of land adjacent to the original tract on his own. I think the original parcel was several hundred acres and bits and pieces got sold off through the years."

"You could be heir to a lot of land, couldn't you?"

"Most of it is mountainside from what I understand. It's supposed to run all the way to the top of the mountain. Not very practical or useful land for a farmer."

"Is there anything else of value on that mountain or in the mountain?"

"What do you mean?"

"What about coal?"

"Not that I am aware."

"Are you sure?"

"Wait a minute. I think I remember hearing my dad and mom talking about signing over the mineral rights to some company that was checking for natural gas."

"Did your mom do that?"

"She said she would lease them the rights. That's what dad told her to do."

"Did anything ever come of that?"

"I don't know. I don't know if Uncle Jim and Aunt Patti agreed to do what mom and dad wanted done."

"Did you ever see any sign of drilling or hear about any being done on the land?"

"No, nothing."

"That was probably nothing, but I'll do some checking. It would have to be filed on record here at the courthouse."

"Did you find a Last Will and Testament for Uncle Jim?"

"I haven't looked for one yet."

"I'm curious to see what his Will has to say, if he had one, since he had never married and had no direct heirs."

"I'll look for it this afternoon and try to start searching the title for the real estate but that will take some time. Doing the title search, I mean."

"What are we going to do now?"

"We're driving out to your property. You said you wanted to check on your belongings stored in the barn, didn't you?"

"Yeah, I forgot about checking after I found you and your poor damaged head."

"I need a break from all of these court records. Let's get some lunch and go visit the barn."

The day was beautiful, just right for a country drive except that they were traveling in separate vehicles.

As funny as it may seem, I wasn't worried about being followed when Tom was around. He made me feel safe, protected, and loved.

I never once glanced in my rearview mirror except to see Tom trailing behind me on the way to the property. The thought of being followed didn't cross his mind either.

When we arrived at the gate at the entrance to the property, I got out of the car, opened it, and we both pulled our vehicles through to the other side. I ran back to lock the gate since I had two good hands and it would be much easier for me to do it.

I parked my car at the top of the hill and climbed into Tom's vehicle that was much higher off the ground. We bounced down the hill and parked near the burned out remains of the house.

"Ellen, I want to see the ashes close up. Let's go take a look."

We walked around what once was a house. Only one of the chimneys remained standing. The wind must have knocked the other down or maybe some vandals did it.

"Look here, Ellen," said Tom pointing at an area that used to be the parlor or formal dining room. "The fire started there. See how much deeper and more severe the burning is?"

"The sheriff said it started in the kitchen."

"Isn't this the kitchen?"

"No, it's the parlor. As far as I knew, there was nothing that would start a fire in there. There were no outlets and the only electricity was from the overhead light."

"Well, it started over there in that corner. Where was the kitchen?"

"The short end of the L-shaped structure. It ran along the base of the hill."

Tom walked to where the kitchen had been. He kicked at a few things, turning over some of the remaining debris for a closer look.

"It started over there. It looks like it was set to me. But I'm no expert. Did the fire marshal come out and have a look?"

"I don't know. You would have to check with the sheriff."

"I will."

Tom pointed at a wooden door built into the hillside that had not been burned. It was within a few feet of the ashes.

"What's that?"

"The root cellar. Grandma kept her canned goods in there. She did most of her own canning from her garden so she needed a cool place to store the goods. The root cellar kept things cool in the summer and usually didn't freeze in the winter because it was dug into the ground like a cave."

"Have you checked it out?'

"No, I never gave it a thought."

"I'll work on trying to get this padlock off. Why don't you go to my car and get my flashlight? It's in my glove box."

I walked away slowly as I glanced back at what Tom was doing. He had picked up a reasonably strong length of wood and wedged it under the hasp. Then he leaned against it with his body. The wood broke but he still had enough of a piece left to try the same tactic again.

When I returned with his flashlight I saw that he had been successful with his second attempt.

"Tom, I've got the flashlight."

"Good, let's see what's inside."

CHAPTER 24
I WONDER WHAT GOD WOULD SAY

Tom pulled at the door and I stood at the ready with the flashlight. The door was set into the frame tightly and it didn't want to break its seal. He pulled again and it moved ever so slightly. The seal was broken so one more tug should open it completely.

We didn't want the door flying back at us knocking both of us off balance.

Tom pulled a final time and it opened slowly emitting the smells of raw earth and decaying vegetation from the opening.

We stood at the doorway staring in at the darkness until I remembered to turn on the flashlight I was holding in my hand.

I knew there should be jars upon jars of home canned vegetables sitting on those shelves. There weren't nearly as many as I would have imagined there would be.

Baskets of apples were decaying and creating an offensive odor; otherwise, the root cellar was in good shape. The remaining canned vegetables looked edible and good enough to grace anyone's table.

"Ellen, you ought to take these home and use them."

"I guess I should. Maybe I can find something to load them into when we go to the barn. We'll just toss the apples out on the ground by the ashes."

"Did your uncle eat a lot of these vegetables?"

"I didn't think he did, but I could be wrong."

"I saw a shed that we walked past up on the hill slightly. Do you know anything about what's kept in there?"

"Nothing because it wasn't kept locked. But when I was here before, I found evidence that someone had been staying in there."

"What kind of evidence?'

"A pile of old blankets and clothes that looked like they had been used for a bed. I was so scared when I was looking around in there that I didn't linger very long."

"Let's go look inside now."

He led the way like an excited child about to embark on a secret exploration.

I jumped ahead of him so I could pull the door open first.

Big mistake!

I was immediately covered from head to foot with a bucket of wet, grimy ashes.

A booby trap had been set, probably because I had entered the building previously.

"Oh, God, Tom, look at this!" I shouted angrily.

Tom was too busy laughing to notice my anger.

Black, sooty water ran down my face, through my hair, and over my clothes.

I walked over to Tom who was so involved with his laughter that he didn't notice my movement. I reached over to him and pulled him close to me so I could give him a big, black, sooty kiss.

When he realized what I was doing, it was too late. I had blackened him to the point that he matched me making us appear to be a couple of giant-sized black bookends.

The kiss led to more, much more. We located some tall grass near the old shed and made love. The excitement of everything that had been happening around us made the adrenaline flow as well as the love. Both of us were a black, sooty mess but that didn't matter because we were in love. When we both had reached our climax together, we fell back staring at the sky.

"I wonder what God would say about everything that's been happening?" I asked Tom as I gazed at the puffy, white, cotton ball clouds floating across the intensely blue sky.

"I'm sure he already knows. He wouldn't have given you more than you could handle, Ellen. He has as much faith in you as I do."

"Tom, I hear a car," I whispered to him apprehensively.

"I hear it, too. Can you tell where it is?"

"No, the sounds sort of bounce around down in this little valley. That's why I had a hard time finding you when you were hit on the head."

"Could it be the lady who lives over there on the hill?" he asked as he pointed toward my cousin's house.

"What time is it?"

"About three."

"She doesn't get home from work until after five. I didn't see her car when we laid down here. She's the only one in the world that could see us here."

"It sounds like it's right over our heads."

"They must be going to her house. Her driveway circles around the hillside."

"Take a look, Ellen. Is that her car?"

"No," I said as I glanced towards my cousin's house where I saw the car turning around in front of the house.

"Do you think they saw us?"

"I hope not. Maybe the shed and the tree that we're lying under blocked the view."

The car drove around the hill back in the same direction from which it had come. Then it stopped. I could no longer hear the engine running so I guessed it had been parked near my car at the top of the hill.

From our position on the slope beside the old shed, I could see the hillside that the stranger would have to walk down. He wouldn't have been able to see Tom's car from the circular trip around the top of the hill because it had been parked on the slope pointing down the hill towards the barn. It was blocked from view by the shed and some trees.

When I popped my head up above the tall weeds, I could see that the car was a sports utility vehicle or SUV and that the driver was walking down the hill hanging close to the weeds that were overhanging the fence that surrounded the garden patch.

"Look, over there," I said as I pointed at the man.

"Do you recognize him, Ellen?"

"No, I don't know who it is because I can't see him clearly. He's just too far away."

The man sneaked down the hillside up next to the fence until he got to a position where he could see Tom's car. He ducked down further towards the ground and walked near Tom's car. He removed something from his pocket along with a pen. He wrote down Tom's plate number, then he turned and fled up the hill.

I couldn't see his license plate. We were too far away. He seemed to have a brightly colored bumper sticker on the left side of his rear bumper and one that was white with black letters on the right side. The SUV was black and it was so clean it sparkled in the bright sunlight.

"He's leaving, Tom."

"I don't think he'll be back anytime soon. Let's go check on your stuff in the barn."

We climbed down the slope above the shed and crossed the yard to the wagon path that led to the barn.

We were no longer the care free, happy-go-lucky couple that we were when we made love in the tall grass. Now we were nervous and uneasy as we glanced around looking for that other shoe that was going to drop on our heads.

When we reached the barn we discovered that the lock had been broken off the door. My furniture inside had been spread out so that it could be used. My belongings were no longer piled almost to the roof in boxes.

Someone had been using my furniture while living in the barn.

"You didn't leave it like this, did you, Ellen?"

"No, I didn't," I said as I looked around to see if anything was damaged or missing.

"Someone's living here."

"Looks like that to me."

"Do you know who?"

"Not unless it's one of Uncle Jim's teenagers. How are we going to find out who it is?" I asked as I looked at the newly created home.

"We need to get rid of the cars so he can't see them parked here. Then we can come inside and wait for him to come home."

"Let's do that tomorrow, Tom. I need a shower. I'll grab a couple of my old bed sheets from one of my packed boxes so we can cover the front seats of the cars. I wouldn't want to get this mess all over the car. I don't know if it can be washed off."

We drove back to the tiny trailer and climbed into the tiny shower together where we washed each other and performed the acts of long lost lovers.

CHAPTER 25
MEETING BOBBY STEPHENS

Saturday arrived with a banging at my front door. I shook Tom to awaken him then I jumped out of bed to see who was beating on my door.

"One minute, please!" I shouted as I tied my robe over my naked body.

The banging continued.

I looked out the front window and saw the sheriff standing outside near his vehicle. A deputy must have been banging on the door.

"What do you want?" I shouted through the door.

"Open up or we'll break it down," shouted the deputy.

I slid the chain lock off and turned the lock in the doorknob.

"What's the problem?" I asked angrily.

"There's been a report of a domestic disturbance."

The sheriff followed behind the deputy as he entered the small trailer.

"There's been a mistake. There hasn't been any kind of disturbance here."

"Are you alone?"

"You know I'm not alone, sheriff."

"Tell him to come in here."

I walked to the bedroom door, "Tom, it's the sheriff answering a domestic disturbance call."

Tom had partially dressed throwing on a pair of jeans and a shirt.

"Who called," Tom asked the sheriff.

"It was anonymous. Don't know who did it. They didn't give a name and it didn't show up on the caller identification system."

"That's convenient, isn't it?" asked Tom with a grin.

"Who are you?" asked the sheriff as he looked at Tom.

"You know who he is. You've already checked him out," I said with obvious irritation coloring my words.

"What are you doing here?" asked the sheriff again looking directly at Tom.

"I just finished making love to this lovely lady."

The statement shut the sheriff up. Both he and the deputy stood staring at Tom.

I felt myself blush but I grinned broadly and waited for the sheriff to ask me to verify Tom's statement.

"There must have been a mistake. Might have been a crank call. We'll get out of here as long as there is nothing wrong."

They turned quickly and let themselves out the door.

I started giggling and Tom started laughing with me as soon as he saw the sheriff and deputy drive away.

"I guess he wasn't expecting an honest answer," said Tom as he hugged me close to him.

"He sure got one."

"Ellen, let's pack up a couple of sandwiches and go see who's living in your barn and why?"

We took my car that we parked on the other side of the creek at the end of the wagon path that passed the barn as it meandered to the road. We locked the car, climbed the fence, and jumped from protruding rock to protruding rock to get across the creek without getting our feet wet. We would get wet regardless because of the grass and weeds we had to tread through without soaking them in the creek.

We tried to sneak up the path to the barn. We stood outside the structure and listened for any sounds of movement inside.

Either the trespasser wasn't inside the barn or he was asleep. It was a judgment call so we entered the barn with the hopes that the former assumption was true. I really didn't want to walk into the barn and awaken the stranger.

We walked softly when we entered the barn, which seemed kind of silly after we heard the loud squeak the door hinges made.

Tom's eyes rapidly checked the right side of the barn while I focused on the left side only.

We saw no one so we closed the door behind them and walked to the sofa where we would while away the time waiting for him to make an expected appearance. Hopefully, neither one of us would be chased or cracked over the head while we waited.

Nature was making herself felt by filling my bladder to capacity and beyond. I had to do something about the pressure soon, very soon.

I walked around inside the barn checking in a couple of stalls. The trespasser had devised his own bathroom facilities by placing a pot with a lid inside a stall along with a roll of toilet paper. At least, my trespasser was trying to be civilized.

Tom was sitting on the sofa dozing slightly and I was in the bathroom stall when I heard the barn door open.

The intruder walked in without a care in the world while I hid in the bathroom stall ready to spring at him if need be.

Tom continued to doze on the sofa as I tried to sneak out of the stall to get between the intruder and the door.

As soon as I was in position, Tom sprang from his dozing position and I rushed forward from the back. We had the intruder sandwiched between us.

He was young, a teenager, who was so frightened that he didn't make a move.

"Who are you?" he shouted in a high-pitched, frightened voice.

"I own the place," I replied angrily. "Who are you?"

"I'm Bobby."

"Bobby who?'

"Bobby Stephens."

"What are you doing here living in this barn?"

"I didn't have any place else to go."

"What about your parents? Your family?"

"They don't want me around. That's why I was living here."

"Why don't they want you home? How old are you?"

"I'm sixteen, old enough to be on my own. I was too much trouble to them. I was an embarrassment. They were ashamed of me. I'm old enough to take care of myself."

"What did you do?" asked Tom as he joined in on the questioning.

"I didn't do nothing, but I was accused of stealing a car and breaking into my uncle's house."

"If you didn't do it, who did?"

"I don't know," he answered as he looked at his feet.

"Were you arrested?" questioned Tom.

"No, my uncle told the sheriff it was a mistake and that nothing was missing."

"Why?" asked Tom.

"He didn't want the son of his brother to go to jail. But, I didn't do it."

"You can't stay here. There's no electricity, no water, and it will start getting cold at night."

"Fine, I'll leave today. I just need to get some things together and put all this stuff back the way I found it."

"Are you the one who chased me all over the place on two different occasions?'

"Not twice, I swear. I did chase you once because I was trying to scare you away."

"Did you hit me over the head earlier this week?" asked Tom loudly.

"No, I wouldn't do that. I wouldn't hurt anybody."

"Do you know who did it?" probed Tom.

Again Bobby looked at his feet when he answered, "No."

"Yesterday, there was a man who parked an SUV at the top of the hill and sneaked down where he saw Tom's car parked. Do you know who that could be?'

"No," he answered but he was glancing down when he said it.

"Was that man looking for you, Bobby?" asked Tom.

"I don't know what you're talking about," Bobby replied sullenly.

CHAPTER 26
KEEP IT IN THE FAMILY

We helped Bobby box my things and stack them up in the middle of the barn. I kept my hammer out so we could fix the hasp on the door and lock everything back up. Bobby had been forced to move the hasp to get inside the barn.

When we were in the car, Bobby started the conversation.

"You're the one: the niece from Ohio, aren't you?"

"Yes, but I live here now."

"Jim told me you'd come and take the place away from me. He left me the land, you know."

"Did he have a will?" asked Tom.

"I guess so. Jim told me he would leave me this place all legal like."

"I'll check the courthouse on Monday. It's Saturday and the courthouse is closed today," said Tom as he tried to reassure me.

"Why would he leave the land to you?" I asked appearing skeptical.

"He said he wanted to keep it in the family."

"Meaning what? Whose family? I'm family."

"Jim's family, I guess. He said he was a Stephens. He said he could prove it."

"How could he prove it?"

"I don't know. He never told me."

My mind was spinning.

"Who was Jim's father? Was he my grandfather also? Was someone trying to hurt Bobby? Or were they after me? The man who sneaked down the hill knew my car was parked there. Was he after me? Did he know Bobby was living in the barn?" continued the mind questions inside my head.

I had so many questions and Bobby was confusing the issue even more than it already was. I remembered the photographs I had in my handbag. I pulled them out and held them in front of Bobby.

"Do you know who any of these people are?" I asked as I quickly flashed them in front of him.

"No," he replied but his eyes told me differently.

"Are you hungry, Bobby?"

"A little, I was planning to trap a rabbit and cook it over a fire."

"Have you been eating the vegetables in the root cellar?"

"Yeah, I found Jim's key ring."

"Is McDonald's okay?"

"Sure, that's fine."

We all ordered dinner to go and took it to the small trailer that was going to be even smaller now with another added presence.

When we walked into the trailer, Bobby saw all the papers scattered about that had come out of the old wooden trunk.

"Where did all of this stuff come from?"

"We found it in the corncrib."

"It was Jim's."

"I know. We're trying to find out who killed him and why? Do you know anything about it?"

He was gazing at his feet again when he answered, "No".

I knew he was lying but I didn't want to pressure him too much, not yet anyway. I wanted him to start to trust us a little so he would be willing to talk to us on his own.

"Well, everybody, let's eat."

The telephone rang and startled all of us. No one had been calling me except Tom and he was right there with me.

"Hello," I said apprehensively into the speaker.

"Ellen, this is Maggie."

"Oh, hi, how are you?"

"I'm calling to let you know that I found the little piece of paper with the license number of the car, the SUV, that had been parked in my way."

"Great, let me get a pencil."

"It's 7888JD. I don't know whom it belonged to. If it helps in finding Jim's killer, please let me know."

"You'll know. Jim's killer will be all over the front page of the newspaper someday. That's where I hope and pray it will be."

"Goodbye, Ellen. Come by the house again when you get a chance."

"Thanks. I really appreciate your help and your invitation," I said before I hung the receiver onto its cradle.

"Bobby, do you know who has the license number 7888JD?" I asked not really expecting an answer.

"Yeah."

"Who?"

"My uncle."

"Why would he be visiting Uncle Jim?"

"Checking on me, I guess," he replied as he gazed at the floor.

Tom and I steered clear of the subject that was most on our minds. We asked Bobby no more questions that evening about Uncle Jim's death or about anything related to the property.

When bedtime rolled around after an evening of cable movies for Bobby's sake, Tom went to my bedroom and I spread clean linens and blankets on the sofa for Bobby.

"When I get up in the morning, Bobby, I want you to be here. No sneaking off into the night. Do you understand?"

"Yes, ma'am."

"If the man I saw was after you, I don't want you to have to deal with him alone. If he was after me, I'm sure he knows where I live. I'll have you and Tom to protect me in the same way that Tom and I will protect you."

Bobby smiled and sat himself down on the clean linens.

"If you want to take a shower, help yourself. Put your dirty clothes in the laundry room and I'll wash them first thing in the morning. If you don't have any clean clothes, I'm sure Tom will loan you something to sleep in, okay?"

"The only clothes I have with me are what I'm wearing."

"Tom, do you have something Bobby could sleep in?" I said to the closed bedroom door.

He walked out of the room carrying a pair of pajamas. He grinned at Bobby and said, "I don't think I'll need these."

Bobby took his shower, piled his clothes in the laundry room, and settled down on the sofa for a restful night's sleep.

I wondered how long it had been for Bobby not to have to be on constant guard listening for footsteps in the night when he slept in the barn. Before the barn, he probably slept in the shed where I ran into him.

When I crawled into bed, Tom had not a stitch of clothing on his body.

"I told you I didn't need the pajamas," he whispered to me.

"Didn't need underwear either, did you?"

"They would only get in the way."

We loved each other slowly, quietly so as not to disturb Bobby. When we were sated with sex, we whispered to each other.

"Tom, when do you have to go back home?"

"Why? You trying to get rid of me?"

"No, never. I love you, Tom. And I love loving you. I don't want it to ever end."

"It doesn't have to end, Ellen."

"Good, I never want you to leave."

"Do you know why it doesn't have to end?"

"If you move in with me permanently, it doesn't have to end."

"No, I don't want to do just that, Ellen. I will move in with you but I want you to marry me, too. We need to make it legal. I am a lawyer, you know."

"Are you sure you want me to marry you?"

"Why would you ask that?" he whispered as he pulled me closer to kiss me long and hard.

"With all the trouble I've been having, I don't want it to bleed over into your life."

"It already has. Put your hand down there. Feel what you do to me. I've never had two of these so close together in my life," he said as he placed my hand on his growing erection.

"Don't ever leave me, Tom," I whispered as he rhythmically pushed in and out of me causing me to have to stifle moans of pleasure.

"They would have to drag me away kicking and screaming," whispered Tom as he kissed me to quiet the moans.

When Tom rolled over to his side of the bed, he immediately fell asleep with a satisfied smile on his beautiful face.

I lay awake wondering what was going to happen next. I didn't want to lose Tom. I didn't think I had ever been as happy as I was at that moment in my life.

Tom made my problems feel small, but lying awake worrying increased their size to reality.

I had two new men in my life: Tom and now Bobby. Tom would help me struggle through, but we both would have to help Bobby.

"Did Uncle Jim tell Bobby he would leave him the property? If he did, I certainly couldn't take it away from him. Bobby and I could share the land. We both needed a place to live that belonged to us. Bobby could have his house and I could have mine," I rationalized.

I looked at Tom and wondered where he lived. What kind of a house did he have? I was sure it wasn't a tiny trailer. Was he still living with his parents since he wasn't married?

'Oh my God,' I thought, 'is he married? Has he ever been married? I never thought to ask.'

I scooted down in the bed inching my body closer to his so I could feel his strength.

His arm problem was a birth defect. I could tell that from looking at it. Was that the reason he never married? Was he afraid he would pass it on to the next generation?

His arm was no problem for me because once I got over the initial shock of discovering the problem, it no longer existed in my eyes and in my dreams.

I loved Tom and he was my knight in shining armor, my hero.

I fell asleep watching my knight scoop me up and carry me away.

CHAPTER 27
GOING TO CHURCH

At seven o'clock I sprang from my bed. I needed to wash Bobby's clothes so we could go to church, to Preacher Johnson's church.

I wasn't going to take no from either of them. It wasn't up for discussion. We were all going to church to let everyone know in that tiny town that we were God-fearing people, too.

All of us were going to go including Bobby, especially Bobby.

I wanted the Stephens family to know that he was with us and that I intended to keep it that way.

"Isn't this a quick decision?" asked Tom who seemed to be agitated by the idea.

"Yes, it is, but it's got to be done," I answered hurriedly as I prepared breakfast.

"I'm not even of the same denomination as that church. I'd rather go to a different one."

"I'm not of the same denomination either, but it doesn't matter. There are small minded people in this small town that need to know that they aren't going to railroad us, any of us," I added as I looked at Bobby.

"Ellen, all I've got are these raggedy old blue jeans," said Bobby.

"That's good enough. We're dressing for God, remember that. He knows what we can afford to wear."

Bobby shrugged his shoulders and ate his breakfast. I was sure he had attended church in the past and the idea was not strange to him.

"Tom, I know you think I'm crazy and I might be. I think these people need to see us together, see us in church, so they know we don't plan to pull up stakes and run."

"Do you want me to wear my jeans, too?" he asked with a smile.

"If you want to. Then Bobby won't feel out of place. It's up to you though."

"I'm wearing my jeans and a nice shirt with a leather jacket. Okay with you?"

"Great," I said as I giggled. "You look so darn sexy in that. You'll make all the women hate me because I have you."

I did some quick patching on Bobby's jeans, and then I put on my denim dress so I would blend in with my guys.

We drove through town in Tom's car, leaving my car parked in front of the trailer.

We found a parking space next to a black SUV with bumper stickers. One of the stickers was brightly colored on the left side and one bumper sticker was black and white on the right side of the bumper. It looked like the same vehicle that had driven all around the property when Tom and I were at Dry Branch.

We walked through the front doors of the church with our heads held high.

As soon as we entered the church, the congregation became silent. No noise of any kind could be heard except our footfalls on the carpet.

We all plastered smiles on our faces and nodded in recognition of all of the staring glances cast in our direction.

As soon as we found a seat, the whispers rippled through the room.

"I think we caused a little stir," I whispered to Tom who had all he could do to keep himself from laughing.

"A little stir, what do these people think you have done? An ax murderer would get a better reception than you're getting here and now."

"I know," I said sadly.

Bobby watched people. He knew some of them knew him and that he hadn't been living at home.

"Ellen, why don't these people like you?" he whispered as he continued to look around.

"I don't know, Bobby. This is the first time I've been to this church. The only people I know who are in attendance are you, Tom, and Preacher Johnson. I haven't done anything to anybody, but they all think I'm guilty of something really, really bad."

"That's not fair, Ellen. They haven't given you a chance."

"It was that way with you, wasn't it? They found you guilty of something you didn't do before they even talked with you. That's how you were accused of stealing your uncle's car, wasn't it?"

"I didn't do it, Ellen."

"I know how you feel, Bobby."

Some of the looks I was receiving were filled with curiosity. Some looks were innocent and unknowing. A couple of harsher stares seemed to be filled with hatred. I could feel those hate filled eyes boring into me searching for my heart to stop it from beating.

Preacher Johnson did not acknowledge my presence as he told me he would do. He was one of those people that cast a harsher, meaner glance in my direction.

We sat through the long-winded sermon which I felt had been aimed at Tom, Bobby, and me when our presence became known. Preacher Johnson seemed to be making the sermon up as he progressed through the preaching which indicated that he had changed it from his prepared format.

"Preacher, I thought you were planning to cover a different topic in your sermon," said a smartly dressed lady in front of the three of us as we waited to get through the door and out into the fresh air.

"I was, Mrs. Leftwich, but I felt really moved by the Spirit of God to speak about the lustful sins of men and women."

"It was a little strong, wasn't it? You certainly left no doubt about what would happen to those participating in sex out of wedlock," questioned Mrs. Leftwich.

"Take my word for it, Mrs. Leftwich, there was a good reason for the sermon," he said as he tried to hurry her along her way out the door.

By the time we had reached Preacher Johnson, he had turned away from us and was talking to people who were standing behind him.

"Wait a minute," I whispered to my handsome escorts. "We'll wait until he turns back around here to speak to us."

We stood on the steps in front of God's house waiting for the man of God to acknowledge us and thank us for attending the service dedicated to God.

Tom and Bobby were becoming uncomfortable standing on the topmost step as people from below gazed up at us. Our audience was obvious about the fact that none of them were going to leave until they saw the outcome of the confrontation.

I didn't want a confrontation.

I wanted an explanation.

I tapped Preacher Johnson on the shoulder.

He ignored me and started to turn to go back inside the church.

I clutched his arm, which made him stop his forward movement completely.

"Miss Hutchins," he said as he turned towards me with obvious disdain.

"Preacher Johnson, I would like a word with you," I said with determination.

"I'm sorry, Miss Hutchins, I don't have time to speak to you right now."

"Oh, I think you do. You're doing an admirable job of leading your flock, you know."

"What are you talking about?"

"Your apparent hatred of me is spreading through your entire congregation."

"I don't hate you, Miss Hutchins. I don't like the way you and your family have lived their lives to date."

"What gives you the right to judge me, Preacher Johnson, or have you taken over God's duties."

The red heat of anger pulsed through Preacher Johnson until all he could do was sputter at me.

"Now, if you've got a moment or two, Preacher Johnson, I need to talk with you. I need to find out why all these people hate me. I need to find out what they know about this whole situation. I need to find out why people are trying to hurt us, perhaps even kill us.

"Tom and I are both strangers to this town. Bobby, here, standing beside me is an outcast. Bobby may know what's going on but he can't or won't tell us. I'm sure he's afraid of the repercussions.

"I want some answers and I'm starting with you, Preacher Johnson. My next step will be a visit with Sheriff Dunsmore. The third step will take me to Bobby's family.

"If you don't want to help me then I will understand that you are one of the biggest hypocrites that ever proclaimed to be a man of God.

"Will you talk to me? Will you tell me what's going on?"

I had taken on a harsh look, also. I wasn't begging for an answer. I was demanding one.

We stared at each other for a few, very long, moments.

CHAPTER 28
I'LL TELL YOU WHAT I KNOW

"Will you be home later today, Miss Hutchins?"

"I will be home anytime you want me to be there."

"About two o'clock, I'll drop by your place at about two o'clock. I'll tell you everything I know then."

"That's all I'm asking."

When it became obvious that there were going to be no fireworks verbally or physically, the crowd members, that were gathered around the bottom of the steps, decided to break up and go their separate ways.

Tom, Bobby, and I walked down the steps with big, fake smiles on our faces. No matter how much their cruel treatment hurt me, I wasn't going to let them, the flock of human sheep, see the pain.

"Let's stop by the grocery store so I can buy something to cook. I have a feeling this is going to be a long day."

I grabbed a roast, some potatoes, carrots, celery, and onions. At least, we were going to eat good at dinnertime. For lunch, we would eat bologna sandwiches and potato chips. I didn't want a big meal before Preacher Johnson arrived. I was afraid his words of explanation might make me sick.

When we arrived at the trailer, everything looked fine from the outside view. When I entered the trailer, I discovered how wrong I was.

Everything was turned over and scattered. Whoever had been in my home wasn't trying to destroy anything, but it was painfully obvious that they were searching for something.

The box of old papers had been emptied back onto the floor. The separate piles I had painstakingly sorted were mingled and mixed.

I ran to my bedroom and looked inside the closet towards the back as far as I could reach and found the box of papers I had set aside for further reading. They hadn't found the box. I knew that what they were searching for was in that box.

I ran to the breaker box where I had hidden my recorded tapes. When I opened the metal door to the box, I found the tapes securely fastened to the inside of the breaker box.

'We should have stayed home and not attended church,' I thought as I looked at the mess. 'I said we had to go. I had to have my way.'

I checked the front door and it didn't look like anybody had jimmied the lock. When I glanced at the back door, I saw the chair was not wedged under the doorknob. The door facing looked like it had taken a beating but the lock mechanism was fine. They probably used the key they made to let themselves inside my tiny trailer and forcefully pushed the chair out from under the knob.

The back door was hidden from view from anywhere near the front of the trailer. You couldn't see the back door from either side of the trailer or the front. You had to walk completely around to the back of the trailer to see the door at all. No one passing by in a car would have seen a person breaking into my home.

Tom and Bobby helped me straighten the mess so they could eat their bologna sandwiches for lunch.

"Bobby, did you get enough to eat?" I asked as I started to clear the plates and cups.

"Yes, ma'am. I had plenty."

"Don't you think it's about time you started talking to me? You heard me tell Preacher Johnson what I thought about his actions. Do you want me to get started on you?"

188

"No, ma'am. I'll tell what I know. It's not much. I don't know how or if it can explain the bad things that are happening to you."

"Tom, if you and Bobby will go into the living room and get comfortable, I'll finish this," I said as I wrapped the leftover bologna.

I turned on the coffeepot for the fresh coffee that I was going to need and I joined my guys in the living room.

Before I could tell Bobby to begin his explanation, there was a knock at the door.

When I looked out to see who was standing on my porch, I saw Preacher Johnson and a woman whom I guessed to be his wife.

"You're early," I said as I asked them to come into my tiny trailer.

"This is Arlene, my wife. I asked her to come with me today. I hope you don't mind but I felt I needed some support of the moral kind to face you and your friends."

"I'm sorry you feel that way, Al," I said as I called him by his informal first name to remind him that once upon a time we were on better terms. I turned toward his wife and extended my hand, "May I call you Arlene?"

She shook my hand and nodded her head in agreement.

I pointed to Tom and introduced him as my fiancé, my friend, and my lawyer. I introduced Bobby as my newfound friend.

"What gives, Al? Why am I being treated like a leper?"

"From what I understand, Ellen, this goes back to your grandmother and your Uncle Jim," he said as he glanced at this wife for reassurance.

"Why am I being blamed for their actions?" I asked sullenly.

"Because you are who you are and you pose a threat to the equilibrium of this small town."

"What threat?"

"You'll see, in due time, you'll see."

"I hope so. I don't understand anything about what's going on here,"

"Your grandmother had a reputation and it wasn't a good one. I didn't know her, only that she had all of her children out of wedlock. She was an outcast and, from what people have told me, she remained an outcast until the day she died.

"Your Uncle Jim wasn't liked. He brought that on himself because, as I told you before, he was a loner and a recluse. He acquired the reputation of being a scavenger who would take anyone's castoffs no matter what it was. Sometimes he would appear like clockwork on certain days to gather his treasures which consisted of the trash of others."

"We all knew he was a collector. You could see that the first time you stepped into his house," I said as I tried to get him past that part of Uncle Jim's life.

"Yes, but did you know that he went through people's trash gathering information that he could use against them?"

"No, why would he do that?" I asked with a hint if disbelief.

"He was looking for something from a particular family," he said as he looked at Bobby. "He wanted information about your family, Bobby. He was interested in your uncle."

Bobby cast his eyes to the floor where he stared at his feet.

"Ellen, your Uncle Jim claimed Bobby's grandfather was his own father. It seems that your grandmother was the whore of Richard County. That's the description she was branded with for loving Bobby's grandfather. As far back as anyone can remember, the only lover she had was Zack Stephens.

"Anyway, Jim Thompson wanted the truth about his mother who he claimed was not a whore and his father, Zack Stephens, to be known and acknowledged."

"Okay, I understand that much. I knew my grandmother had her three children out of wedlock. I didn't know who she was sleeping with. So, now I'm a distant relative of Bobby's family."

"It seems," continued Preacher Johnson, "that certain members of the Stephens family didn't approve of the influx of bastard children."

"Why?"

"It besmirched the legacy and good name of Zack Stephens. If the truth came out, you, your brother, and your two cousins could stake a claim to some of the family fortune or so they thought."

"I don't want their money- no way, no shape, no how," I said angrily.

"You might not want it, but other members of your family could file a claim."

"Uncle Jim was trying to do what he thought was right by his mother and my grandmother. Why was that so wrong?"

"It wasn't wrong. It was just dangerous."

"Bobby," said Preacher Johnson as he looked into the frightened eyes of the teenager, "why were you living with Jim Thompson?"

Bobby squirmed in his seat. He didn't want to answer the question.

"All right, if you won't tell us, then I'll tell you. You were sent to stay with Jim Thompson as a family spy."

Bobby's head snapped up and denial was on the tip of his tongue unsaid.

"Bobby, do you know who started all the bad talk about Jim Thompson being a homosexual?" probed Preacher Johnson.

Bobby shook his head negatively.

"Sure you do, Bobby. Your uncle started it. Jeremiah Stephens said Jim Thompson was gay and that since you were, too, he was glad you went to live with him."

"No, that's not true! I'm not gay!" shouted Bobby vehemently.

"But it is, Bobby. I heard him say those very words."

I watched Bobby fighting the angry tears glistening in his eyes.

"Leave Bobby be for a few minutes," I admonished the preacher. "Tell me how this affects me, Tom, and Bobby in the here and now."

"Think about it, Ellen."

"I've done all the thinking and rationalizing I can do for now. I need explanations."

"Everybody knows what your grandmother did. Everybody knows that your Uncle Jim was a pervert. It stands to reason that what you are doing now is carrying on the family tradition."

"What am I doing to carry on that tradition?'

"Why, you're sleeping with a man you're not married to. You have a homosexual living in your house. These acts are contrary to the teachings of the Lord."

Arlene leaned over and patted her husband's knee in a gesture of reassurance and agreement.

"Get out of my house, both of you holier-than-thou hypocrites. Like I said before, who gave you the right to judge me?"

Tom stood between me and the preacher and his wife. He was afraid I would take a swing at one of them, if not both of them.

"Like the lady said, you'd better get out of here. I don't think I can control her much longer. I don't think I even want to try," said Tom as he moved from the role of spectator to participant.

Bobby was angry and near tears again. Rather than punch the stupid people that were standing in front of me, I threw my arms around Bobby to show him that I truly cared.

Never again would I call him preacher. That was a respected title that belonged to a deserving man. Al and Arlene were common, not special in any way.

CHAPTER 29
I'M PROUD TO KNOW YOU

After the departure of Al and Arlene, I collapsed onto the sofa and cried. Tom did his best to console me but I didn't want to be consoled. I wanted an apology from the world for the way I was being treated, for the way Bobby was being treated, and for the way Tom was being treated.

"Bobby, I'm glad you're a relative, but you might not feel the same way about me."

"Sure I do, Ellen. I couldn't be any happier about that. I'm proud to know you."

"Tom, what about you?"

"I love you, Ellen. Of course I'm proud," he said as he hugged me to his strong, manly body.

"I'm going to put the roast on to cook. Then we can look at those papers piled up in the corner."

Tom went outside for some air and Bobby tagged along with him.

I bustled around the kitchen pretending that the cut of meat I was trying to season and sear in the Dutch oven was important. After the searing of the meat, I added water to the pot to make a good beef broth. I threw in the chunks of peeled and pared vegetables and left the kitchen while the meat and vegetables cooked at a slow simmer.

I sat on the floor and started reading each and every piece of paper I picked up.

There was a little bit of everything spread in front of me from grocery lists, to bills of sale for cattle, to copies of court records.

Attached to one list of items that appeared to be a list of personal possessions was an aging, yellowed envelope that had once been sealed but was now only folded closed. The paper in the envelope was apt to break and crack if I pulled too much so I handled it very carefully as I slid out the contents so I could read it.

The paper I removed from the envelope was a heavier grade, with a parchment quality, and because it hadn't been exposed to handling and the air as much as the envelope, it looked much newer.

When I first glanced at it, I couldn't comprehend what I was reading. I stopped myself about half way through the document and then began again.

By the time I had finished reading after starting the second time, I was crying.

It was a marriage license. Grandma Molly Thompson was married to Zack Stephens.

It appeared to be the original document and for whatever reasons known only to her and Zack, it was never recorded in the courthouse records.

When Tom and Bobby returned, I proudly displayed my discovery.

"My grandmother was married to Zack Stephens."

"She couldn't have been," said Bobby in defense of his name and everything he believed in. "He was married to my grandmother."

"I'd say the sly old bastard was married to both women," added Tom. "The family didn't want anyone to know he was a bigamist."

"Grandma must have gone through hell to protect his good name. She must have truly loved him and did so until her last breath. The other alternative would have been that she was so afraid of him that she couldn't let the truth be known. So afraid of him that she was at his beck and call whenever the mood for sex crossed his mind. I hope she loved him more than she feared him.

"Okay, now this little piece of paper explains a lot," I said as I held the marriage license in my hand.

"Like what?" asked Bobby.

"It explains why the old school house and the home place were burned. Also, it tells me why Uncle Jim was killed. What it doesn't tell me is who did it? And why you were involved?" I said as I turned to Bobby.

Bobby looked at his feet again to avoid my probing eyes.

"Look at me, Bobby. Tell me why you are in the middle of this whole mess?"

"I can't, Ellen. I would get in really big trouble if I told anybody."

"You've got to tell me, Bobby. You're the missing key."

"If I tell, I'll go to jail."

"For what? Being related to Zack Stephens?" asked Tom with a smile.

"No, for stealing a car."

"You said you didn't do it," added Tom.

"I didn't do it but I wouldn't squeal on my buddy. The sheriff was really mad about that."

"You said your uncle didn't press charges," I said in response to Bobby's statement.

"The sheriff said my uncle didn't have to press charges if a felony was committed. The state would have me arrested, tried, and convicted, too."

"Is that true, Tom?"

"Yes, it doesn't matter if his uncle presses charges if the theft is reported."

"How did you get out of it?"

"The sheriff knew I was having trouble at home. He asked my mom and dad if it would be all right for me to go live with Jim Thompson for a while because he was so old and feeble and needed help around his place."

"What's that got to do with anything?" I snapped.

"He wanted me to spy on Jim and tell him, the sheriff I mean, what Jim was up to."

196

"Dunsmore did this?" I asked in an unbelieving tone.

"There were two of them, Sheriff Dunsmore and Deputy Martin. They wanted me to tell them where Jim kept his personal papers and such."

"I thought they said Uncle Jim was a homosexual?"

"They knew he wasn't gay. That was just an ugly rumor probably started by my uncle like the preacher said."

"Was the sheriff and his deputy working with your uncle?"

"I think so. But I never told them anything. That's why I had to hide. They were trying to find me to make me tell them where all those papers that belonged to Jim were hidden."

"Are you the one who hid them in the corncrib?"

"Yeah, I thought if I put them in plain sight, they wouldn't find them."

"Were you living with Uncle Jim when the sheriff paid a visit because he was shooting his gun?"

"Yeah."

"Why was he doing that?"

"It was a warning. He knew someone had been snooping around the property that same day. If they were still there, he wanted them to know he would fight for what was his."

"Do you know who has been chasing and following me?"

"I was the first one to chase you. All I wanted to do was scare you away, that's all, I swear."

"Okay, Bobby, I believe you. Who else followed me?"

"Deputy Martin and another one named Deputy Jones."

"Are they involved in this?"

"They just do what the sheriff tells them to do."

"Why is the sheriff doing it?"

"My uncle's paying him."

"You're kidding," said Tom.

"No, my family has a lot of money that they don't want to share with anybody."

"Did Uncle Jim write a new will?" I asked.

"I don't think so. He said he was going to but he got killed."

"Who killed him Bobby?"

"Sheriff Dunsmore."

"Oh, my God," I said as I realized what I had uncovered.

"You can't go to the police, Ellen. The sheriff is the killer."

"I know. I know. Tom, what can we do about this?"

"Bobby, did you see the sheriff kill Jim Thompson?"

"Yes, Jim was sitting in his car with the engine running and he didn't see the sheriff come running down the hill. When the sheriff reached Jim's car, he squatted down low and Jim started to try and get out of the car. The sheriff shot him. Blood was pouring all over the seat where Jim had fallen. The sheriff shoved Jim over towards the passenger side and drove the car down to the barn. He drove inside the barn and shoved Jim out of the car. Then he drove back up to the house."

"What did he do next?"

"Well, I was pretty well hidden, scared to death that he would find me. I knew he would have to kill me so I couldn't talk."

"How long was he in the house?" I asked trying to push him forward.

"Just a few minutes. He looked in every room. I think he was looking for the papers, but when he saw how the house was filled with boxes of junk and all kinds of papers, he left. He had something in his hand like a garbage bag that he threw across the front seat of Jim's car. He had to cover the blood somehow. Then he drove off in Jim's car."

"He's the one that parked the car in the church lot," I said as I was filling in the blanks. "I'm sure the fact that Bobby went to church with us will get back to the sheriff. You can't keep a secret in this town.

"I'm sure he knows by now. He also knows that Bobby is the missing piece that can connect him to Jim and Bobby's uncle."

"What are we going to do, Tom?"

CHAPTER 30
DEADLY SECRETS

Tom led us to the car. We were going to find help.

We drove away from Lebanon towards the next county, which was Stillwell County.

"Ellen, I'm driving us all to the state trooper headquarters in Stillwell. I want both of you to be ready to tell your story to the troopers. I don't think you can do that without risking your lives in Richard County."

"Okay, what then?"

"Warrants will have to be issued and arrests made. There will be some time lag involved. I don't want you or Bobby where they can find you."

"You're scaring me, Tom," I said timidly.

"I hope so. The sheriff will be fighting for his life so if it includes killing you in the fight, one more murder isn't going to matter to him."

"Where will we go?"

"I own a house in Florida. We're going to stay there for a while."

"Florida?"

"I bet you didn't know you were marrying a wealthy man."

"I had no idea. I thought you were doing well as a lawyer, that's all."

"No, it's family wealth. My lawyer skills haven't put my name on the Who's Who of Lawyers List yet. But I'll be there someday."

"What about Bobby?"

"He's a bigger part of this mess than you are. He needs to be protected."

"Hear that, Bobby? We're going to Florida."

Sirens and flashing lights suddenly appeared from nowhere. There was a sheriff's car in front of them as well as one behind them. They had no choice but to pull off to the side of the road.

"Tom, where did those guys come from?" I asked as I tried to cover the fear in my voice.

"That side road we just passed. One pulled out in front of me and the second one jumped right in line behind."

"What do you think they want?" I asked apprehensively.

"I don't know, but I don't think it's anything good."

We watched as a deputy sheriff exited his car and drew his gun.

"What's he got his gun out for?" asked a frightened Bobby.

"I don't know, Bobby. Just do what they tell you. Don't give him any reason to use that gun because I think he's looking for one, a reason I mean."

"Get out of the vehicle, now. Get out, now?" shouted the deputy when he saw the occupant of the second sheriff's car walk up next to him. The second man also had his gun drawn and ready to fire.

"Sheriff, what's the problem?" asked Tom as he directed his question to the second man.

"Do as you're told. Get out of the vehicle, now," responded Sheriff Dunsmore.

Tom climbed out of the car on the driver side. I exited on the passenger side followed by Bobby who climbed from the back seat on the passenger side.

"Get down on the ground," barked the deputy.

"Sheriff, that isn't necessary," said Tom.

"Do as he says. Get down on the ground, now. Don't give me any reason to use this," said the sheriff as he waved his handgun for emphasis.

"Do as he says," said Tom as he got to his knees and then stretched out on the ground.

I got down on the ground next to Tom and Bobby was next to me.

"What's this about, Sheriff Dunsmore?" I asked as I looked up at him.

"I'm arresting you for the murder of Jim Thompson," he said with a smirk.

"You've got to be kidding?" I sputtered.

"You'll find out if I'm kidding or not. We've got plenty of evidence. All three of you were involved in this. All three of you will be tried for a capital crime."

"Tom didn't even know Uncle Jim. Bobby lived with him. He certainly wouldn't hurt Jim. I lived in another state. You know all of this. How can you tell me that there is any kind of evidence saying that we killed Uncle Jim?"

"You need to shut up, now," barked the deputy.

"Martin, get the cuffs on the prisoners and get them into the back of your car," ordered Sheriff Dunsmore.

"What about him? How do I handcuff him?"

"Handcuff the boy and after you get him cuffed then handcuff the lawyer's good arm to the boy's arm. That ought to hold them."

The deputy pulled me up from my position on the ground. Then he helped Tom and Bobby get up because they were handcuffed together.

He led us to the car and he pushed down on my head with one hand as he pushed against my back with his other hand forcing me to climb into the back seat of the vehicle. Next, he pushed Bobby's head down and then Tom's as the two of them awkwardly fell into the car seat because of the handcuffs.

"Can't you take these cuffs off of us so we can sit back in the seat?" asked Tom softly.

"No can do, Mr. Lawyer. You might attempt to escape. It would be a real shame to shoot you if you tried to run. I don't like to shoot people in the back. But I will. I will shoot you in the back if you try to run."

"Where are you taking us?" I asked as I tried to control my voice. I didn't want them to know how scared I was.

"To jail, of course. All killers should be in jail," said the deputy as he started the engine.

Deputy Martin was not trying to drive carefully as he pulled out into the traffic from the side of the road. The force of the movement at such a rapid speed forced us back into the seats against our cuffed hands. Then we were whipped from side to side as he rounded the curves at excessive speed.

We were not being driven to Lebanon. The car was pointed in the opposite direction.

I looked at Tom and I saw determination on his brow. If he had looked at me, at that moment, all he would have seen was fear.

"This isn't the way to jail," said Bobby as he looked past me to the side of the road.

"Shut up, boy."

"He's right. This isn't the way to jail. Where are you taking us?" demanded Tom.

"I'm taking you to a place to be identified by an eyewitness."

"What eyewitness?"

"There was a young boy staying at Thompson's property the day he was killed. He saw you kill Thompson and then dump his body in the barn. Then he saw you drive away in Jim Thompson's car. I guess that was when you parked it at the church."

"Your witness is a liar. He couldn't have seen any of that happen. There was a witness but the real witness saw what actually happened."

"Who's the witness? Who really saw what happened?" demanded Deputy Martin.

"I'm not going to tell you that because then you'll try to get rid of the real witness," said Tom as he baited the deputy into an argument.

"It's the kid, isn't it?" asked Deputy Martin as he glanced into the rearview mirror.

"No, not this kid. Bobby wasn't there that day."

"Then how do you know there wasn't another witness?"

"Because we would have been arrested a long time ago if that were the case."

"What did your witness see? The witness you said was a real one?" continued the deputy.

"He saw who did the shooting."

"He couldn't have. There wasn't anyone there."

"Who told you that? The sheriff?" asked Tom.

"Of course the sheriff told me. He's the one who found the witness who said you did the killing," answered the confused deputy.

"How would he know there wasn't another witness?"

"But there was a witness. We're going to see him. You are going to be identified by that witness."

"I'm not talking about the fake witness, the one the sheriff has paid to identify us. I'm talking about a real witness. How do you know there wasn't a witness that really saw what happened?"

Tom's questions were even hard for me to follow and I knew what was going on.

"The sheriff said Johnny Josephs was the one and only witness."

"How does he know for sure?"

"What do you mean?"

"Unless the sheriff was there in the room with Jim Thompson at the time of the shooting, how would he know for certain that there were no other witnesses?"

"He wouldn't unless he…"

"See what I mean. How can he be so sure?"

"Just shut up. You're getting me confused," whined the deputy.

"Where is this Johnny Josephs?" I asked just to keep the deputy in his confused state of mind.

"Up ahead on the right. There is an old cabin that he has been staying in for the summer. I think he is a homeless boy."

"There was a Johnny that stayed at Jim's for a couple of nights. Jim caught him in a lie and told him to hit the road."

"What did he lie about?" asked the deputy.

"His age, I think. I believe he was older than what he told Jim. He just looked young."

"Is that all?"

"No, he said he had AIDS."

"Are you kidding me?" asked the shocked deputy.

"That's what he told Jim. He also said he was gay and that's why he had AIDS."

"God, no, kid, I hope you're lying to me."

"Well, I'm not. That's what Jim said and he's not alive to ask, is he?"

Suddenly the car pulled off to the side of the road.

"I'm going to turn this car around and take you back to your vehicle. Then I want you three to get into that vehicle and get out of town."

"Why aren't you taking us to see the witness?" Tom asked skeptically.

"The sheriff is waiting there with that witness. At least, that's what he told me he was going to do. I think it's a trap. I think he's planning to kill all three of you and me, too. I don't think I can trust him. He probably doesn't think he can trust me. I think he's right about that. I'm not going to get caught up in this mess any more than I already am."

"Thank you, Deputy Martin. Thank you so much for believing us," I said as I was filled with relief.

The deputy reached into his pocket and pulled out a set of keys that he tossed towards me. Bobby caught the keys in his mouth and held them as I squirmed around in the seat so I could grab the keys in my cuffed hands. I worked the keys around until I could get one into the lock.

"Bobby, can you back up towards me a little so you can turn the key in the lock?"

"I don't know. Tom is still attached to me."

"I'll lean over as much as I can, Bobby. Go ahead and try to unlock that thing," said Tom as he struggled to get as close as possible to the two of us.

"You're almost there, Bobby. I can feel your fingers. Just a little bit more."

"Can you lean in a little?" asked Bobby as he tried to pull himself closer to me.

"I'll try."

"There, I've got hold of the key. Let me try to turn it."

I felt the lock open and the handcuff loosened to allow my wrist to move around a bit.

"You've got it, Bobby. Sit up a little and I'll get my one wrist loose so I can unlock the other wrist. Then I'll get you guys."

I struggled with keys and locks for a few more minutes until we were all three free from the handcuffs.

"We've got company," said Deputy Martin.

Tom and I turned our heads to see another sheriff's car speeding up behind us with sirens blaring and lights flashing.

"What are you going to do?" I asked as I watched the speeding vehicle behind us

"I'm going to radio ahead to Stillwell County. If we can get to the county line before that car catches us or forces us off the road, I'll ask for an escort to the Virginia State Police Headquarters just inside the Stillwell County line."

"How far is it?"

"Couple of miles."

The deputy was trying to talk to the Stillwell County Sheriff's Office Dispatcher as well as steer his speeding vehicle along a narrow, winding, county road.

We weren't able to help him because of the metal mesh that separated the front seats from the back seats. The wire mesh was a safety measure to protect the deputies from their prisoners.

"Were you able to convince the dispatcher that you needed help?"

"I hope so."

A shot rang out and hit the trunk of the vehicle.

"He's shooting at us! The sheriff is shooting at us!" shouted Bobby as he cringed down in the seat.

"He's getting closer. What can we do?" I cried.

"Just get down and stay down," shouted the deputy. "It's not much further ahead."

"He's right behind us," said Tom. "Keep swerving the car," he added with encouragement. "A moving target is harder to hit. I hope he doesn't hit one of the tires. We would probably flip the car if that happened."

Another shot hit the car.

Bobby tried to get onto the floor.

"That's good, Bobby. You get on the floor. Ellen, you get down there on top of Bobby."

"What about you, Tom?"

"I'll get down as far as I can but Deputy Martin needs another set of eyes. He is trying to cover too much territory now without any help."

The back window burst and showered tiny pieces of glass all over them.

"He's trying to pull up beside us. Swerve to your left some more so you can block him. If he gets any closer, we're dead," shouted an anxious Tom.

We felt the car hit the sheriff's car as Deputy Martin swerved to the left. The bang to the right front fender of the sheriff's car forced the sheriff's car off the road and into a ditch.

The flashing lights behind them stopped and we heard no more sirens.

"They're up ahead. The Stillwell County Sheriff is waiting for us. I can see their flashing lights. Just a little further."

The state troopers had a real problem with understanding our story until Sheriff Dunsmore was mentioned as the glue that held it together.

They advised the three of us to disappear from sight for a while for our own safety.

Tom and I married in Florida and when the three of us returned for the trial, we moved into the Walker family home to take our place in the history of Stillwell County, Virginia.

My property in Richard County will be Bobby's land one day. I'll see that he gets it, just as Uncle Jim promised him.

My family really wasn't full of whores and perverts. They were just people who were trying to do the best they could do.

They were simple folk with deadly secrets.

Linda Hudson Hoagland

OTHER BOOKS WRITTEN BY LINDA HUDSON HOAGLAND:

FICTION

ONWARD AND UPWARD

MISSING SAMMY

AN UNJUST COURT

SNOOPING CAN BE HELPFUL - SOMETIMES

SNOOPING CAN BE DOGGONE DEADLY

SNOOPING CAN BE DEVIOUS

SNOOPING CAN BE CONTAGIOUS

SNOOPING CAN BE DANGEROUS

THE BEST DARN SECRET

CROOKED ROAD STALKER

CHECKING ON THE HOUSE

DEATH BY COMPUTER

THE BACKWARDS HOUSE

NONFICTION

90 YEARS AND STILL GOING STRONG

QUILTED MEMORIES

LIVING LIFE FOR OTHERS

JUST A COUNTRY BOY: DON DUNFORD (Edited)

WATCH OUT FOR EDDY

THE LITTLE OLD LADY NEXT DOOR

COLLECTIONS

I AM... LINDA ELLEN (POETRY)

A COLLECTION OF WINNERS (SHORT PROSE)

74296662R00117

Made in the USA
Columbia, SC
11 September 2019